PSYCHIC
ZONE

ALIEN SEA

MATHEW STONE

Hodder
Children's
Books

a division of Hodder Headline plc

Copyright © 1998 Mathew Stone

First published in Great Britain in 1998
by Hodder Children's Books

The right of Mathew Stone to be identified as the Author of
the Work has been asserted by him in accordance with the
Copyright, Designs and Patents Act 1988.

10 9 8 7 6 5 4 3 2 1

A Catalogue record for this book is available from
the British Library

ISBN 0 340 69841 1

Typeset by Avon Dataset Ltd, Bidford-on-Avon, Warks

Printed and bound in Great Britain by
Clays Ltd, St Ives plc

CONTENTS

1   The Ghosts of Penwyn-Mar   1
2   The Watcher on the Shore   18
3   Footprints in the Sand   37
4   Malvaine   54
5   Sailing to Lyonesse   63
6   The Prisoners of Lyonesse   74
7   An Audience with Broderick
    Rune   83
8   Escape Into Danger   95
9   Alien Sea   111
10 Forever Young   136

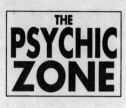

THE PSYCHIC ZONE

1

The Ghosts of Penwyn-Mar

Dateline: Penwyn Mar, Cornwall;
Tuesday 25 August; 11.15.

Evil dwelt at Penwyn-Mar. That was what Colette Russell had always been told, ever since she had first come here to Cornwall as a small child to stay with her Aunt Anne.

Anne to her father, that was. Always Annie to Colette. Her aunt might now be in her late-forties, but there was still something ageless about Aunt Annie. Maybe even childlike. She wasn't really a grown-up, she had told Colette when she was six years old. And now, seven years later, Colette still believed that. Yes, *ageless*: that was what Aunt Annie was.

Of course, Annie didn't believe the stories of the drowned village of Penwyn-Mar, supposedly located some three or four miles out at sea, and she'd always scolded Blaise, the boatkeeper, for filling her young niece's head with such nonsense.

As far as she was concerned, the village she had lived in all her life was Penwyn-Mar, and nowhere else. That was what she said to anyone who asked her; from the day-trippers who travelled the ninety or so miles from Plymouth in search of legends of the Round Table, to the windsurfers who, discovering the magnificent waves near Arthur's Bay, had turned what had once been a tiny fishing village into one of the country's major windsurfing venues.

And, if evil did really dwell at Penwyn-Mar, Aunt Annie would sometimes ask Colette, then why was the village universally acknowledged as one of the healthiest places in all Britain? After all, Jeff Monmouth, the local GP, was famous for spending most of his days down at the local pub, The Smugglers' Retreat, rather than attending to his patients. Not that anyone begrudged him that, because it was a fact that no one ever seemed to get ill in Penwyn-Mar; there hadn't even been an outbreak of flu last year, and no one could remember the last time anyone had anything so serious that it had required hospital attention.

'Maybe they've found the secret of eternal youth,' Colette said as she and her friend, Rebecca, watched the windsurfers down in the bay from their vantage point on top of the cliff. 'They've finally located and tapped into the fountain of youth.'

'Got into good diets and clean living, more like,' Rebecca said. Rebecca Storm was a good-looking red-head a couple of years older than Colette. She'd come originally from New York and, like most natives of that city, possessed a down-to-earth manner which sometimes made Colette uneasy. Colette liked to believe in things which couldn't be explained by any rational reasons. She thought such ideas were romantic and exciting. Rebecca, on the other hand, wouldn't bring herself to consider anything which couldn't be proved by good old-fashioned scientific observation. Despite this, though, the two of them were the greatest of friends.

'This place used to be a fishing port after all,' Rebecca continued. 'After they shut down the last of the tin mines. The locals' diet will be low in both fat and cholesterol. I just wish old Ma Chapman back home at the Institute would serve us up that sort of thing more often.'

'You're no fun,' Colette said, and laughed. She was a short, slim girl with an open face whose closely-cropped blonde hair, designed to give her a tomboyish look, only served to make her appear younger than her thirteen years.

'And as for good living . . .' Rebecca said, and raised her eyes heavenwards in mock despair.

'I know,' Colette agreed. 'Apart from the wind-surfers, Penwyn-Mar isn't the most exciting place to visit at the tail-end of the summer holidays.'

'Don't I know it,' Rebecca said, with feeling. 'No

shops, no clubs, no halfway decent coffee shops . . .'

'No McDonald's,' Colette added longingly.

'Still, it was sweet of Annie to invite us down for a couple of weeks,' Rebecca allowed. 'She's a great person. How old did you say she was?'

'Forty-nine last birthday,' Colette replied. 'Can you believe it – my father took her to EuroDisney to celebrate! Even *I'm* too old for all that Mickey Mouse sort of thing now.'

'Forty-nine,' Rebecca said thoughtfully, as she continued to watch the windsurfers tacking and gybing in the waters of the bay. 'She looks real good for her age. I wouldn't have put her past thirty.'

'See. I told you. The villagers of Penwyn-Mar really *have* discovered the secret of eternal youth,' Colette crowed triumphantly.

'Let's hope Marc doesn't find it then,' Rebecca joked, and pointed to a wet-suited figure down in the bay, trying (unsuccessfully) to raise the sail of his brightly coloured windsurfing board. 'He already acts like a five-year-old. Imagine if he stayed that mental age for the rest of his life!' She giggled as Marc's board overturned once again and he landed in the waters with a splash which even she and Colette could hear from the top of the cliff.

'Don't be too hard on him,' Colette said, trying hard not to giggle herself at Marc's antics in the water. 'He's trying his best.'

'It makes a change from all his tales about spooks out at sea,' Rebecca said, as she and Colette started to walk away from the cliff edge and back towards Penwyn-Mar proper. 'Ever since he heard the stories of the lost village, we haven't been able to shut him up.'

'Ever since we *saw* something as well,' Colette said, and Rebecca shifted uncomfortably in the spot where she was standing.

'It was a figment of our imaginations, nothing more,' she claimed, not entirely convincingly.

'We all of us did see something,' Colette insisted, and reminded Rebecca of their first night at Penwyn-Mar: Shafts of green light, playing about above the water, dancing in the moonlight like so many emerald snowflakes.

'A freak atmospheric effect,' Rebecca said. 'Something like the *Aurora Borealis*.'

'In Cornwall?' Colette asked disbelievingly. Even she knew that the Northern Lights were never seen this far south.

'Well, maybe Saint Elmo's fire,' Rebecca suggested and, in response to Colette's blank look, explained: 'that electric discharge you sometimes see around the mast of a ship.'

Colette wasn't going to be put off now. 'No ships have come around here for years now because of the rocks,' she pointed out. 'Even the fishing boats don't like setting out at night, and they know the waters round here really well.'

Rebecca glowered at Colette. For someone who wasn't a trained scientist, she was being particularly reasonable – and awkward to boot.

'OK, then it was probably something to do with that old lighthouse out at sea,' she said, a little peevishly.

'Pendragon Rock has been abandoned for years now. Some people even claim that the lighthouse is haunted,' Colette said smugly. 'Admit it, Rebecca, those lights we saw out at sea the other night really did come from the ghost village of Penwyn-Mar!'

'For the last time, there is no ghost village of Penwyn-Mar!'

'I wouldn't be so sure of that, Miss Storm,' a cracked voice said from behind them. The two girls jumped with surprise and turned around to see who had crept up on them as silently as a big cat stalking its prey out on the moors. 'Strange things happen at Penwyn-Mar.'

'Blaise, it's you,' Colette said, recognising the burly boatkeeper who had lived in the village longer than she or anyone else could remember. She wondered what he was doing up here on the cliffs when he should be attending to his boats down in the bay.

Old though he might be, Blaise wasn't one to stand still with the passing times. Ever since Penwyn-Mar had become a magnet for windsurfers, he'd made a tidy sum hiring out boards and sails to the young people who flocked to Penwyn-Mar every summer.

'What do you mean, "strange things" happen here at Penwyn-Mar?' Rebecca wanted to know.

'Exactly what I said,' he replied. Blaise was a

man of very few words: most of them enigmatic and baffling.

'Tell us about the village out at sea,' Colette urged him.

'They say that all this place – from the coast to way past the Pendragon Rock lighthouse – used once to be dry land,' Blaise said, with a faraway look in his eyes. 'The people living there were bandits and pirates: evil men. They did terrible things, holding the rest of Penwyn-Mar in terror. One day, however, they went too far, and a curse was brought down on them by the local wise woman. The next day the sea rose, drowning the lost village and all those who lived in her,' Blaise said. 'They were never seen again, although if you listen closely at night then you can hear their screams of terror as the waters rushed in, washing them forever from the face of the Earth.'

Colette shivered, in spite of the warmth of the late-August sun. 'There are so many stories and legends around here,' she said.

'That's right,' Blaise said. 'The old land of Cornwall is a place of mystery and magic. There are other stories too: of terrible hell-hounds that haunt the hills; of water-demons and of men who can turn themselves into sea-creatures; of King Arthur and the Holy Grail.'

'Don't I know it,' Rebecca said resentfully. 'Practically everything around here seems to have an Arthurian connection. There's Arthur's Bay. Grail Hallows Point at the far end of the bay. Ye

Olde Round Table Tea-Shoppe. You can even buy tiny plastic Swords in the Stone! It's refreshing to know that we Americans don't have the franchise on bad taste and tackiness.'

Blaise smiled: Rebecca did have a point. Ever since the legends had spread that Penwyn-Mar might be the final resting place for King Arthur, tourists had been flocking to Penwyn-Mar from far and wide to discover some of the magic of Cornwall for themselves. Blaise didn't mind, however. Ever one to spot a chance to make a quick buck, he'd wasted no time in setting up a souvenir shop – in addition to his other money-making schemes.

'And what do you think, Blaise?' Colette asked. 'Do you really think that King Arthur is buried hereabouts?'

Blaise was evasive. 'Maybe I do and maybe I don't,' he replied. 'There are certain things in this place that can't be explained – even by scientists, like Miss Storm here.'

'What you're really trying to say, Blaise, is that you don't want anything to harm your little money-making schemes,' Rebecca said cannily. 'If the stream of tourists coming into Penwyn-Mar dried up then you'd have no one to sell your tacky souvenirs to, and no one to take on over-priced speedboat trips around the harbour.'

Blaise didn't reply, but smiled at Rebecca in such a complicit way that she knew that she was right. Blaise was a bit of an old rogue, that was certain, but there was also something quite endearing about him too. Rebecca was reminded of some of the hucksters she'd seen on the streets of New York: they'd blag every last cent out of you, but in such a charming way that you didn't really mind at all.

'I'm only ever interested in what I can see and hear with my own eyes and ears,' Rebecca said, sounding a little more pompous than she would have liked. 'Like Blaise said, I *am* a scientist, after all.' She turned back to Colette. 'Are you coming down to the dig now?' she asked her.

Colette sighed. There was nothing she would have liked to do more than stay here with Blaise and listen to his stories of King Arthur and the Holy Grail. Still, she said that, yes, she would accompany Rebecca.

'You going to that fancy archaeological dig?' Blaise asked, in a tone of voice which bordered on disbelief. 'You're both young girls. You need a little excitement in your lives. Why do you want to be around a heap of boring old bones and buildings? I could hire you out a couple of boards – at a very reasonable price, too. I've got a young chap down there who'd give you lesssons.'

Rebecca smiled at Blaise's constant salesmanship. 'Sorry, Blaise,' she said lightly. 'I happen to be interested in "boring old bones". Not that we're likely to find many. It's just the remains of a Fifth Century fort. But it promises to be fascinating.'

Blaise's face fell, but he made one last appeal. 'Then what about you, Colette?' he asked. 'I'm sure your aunt wouldn't mind you hiring a boat.'

Colette shook her head awkwardly, and turned away so that Blaise wouldn't see the embarrassed look in her eyes. 'I can't swim,' she said with shame, and then added: 'Well, not very well anyway.'

Rebecca recognised her friend's embarrassment and gave her a friendly pat on the back. 'C'mon, Colette, that dig won't wait forever, you know!' she said cheerily.

'It has for the past fifteen hundred years,' Colette pointed out as she started to follow Rebecca down the cliff. She stopped and turned to Blaise.

'I've known you all my life,' she reminded him, 'but I've never asked you how old you are.'

'Sixty-one next birthday,' Blaise said casually, and Rebecca and Colette each looked in wonder at the man. He only looked about forty – and a well-preserved forty at that. Perhaps Colette had been right after all. Perhaps the villagers of Penwyn-Mar did indeed possess the secret of eternal youth!

Dateline: Arthur's Bay;
Tuesday 25 August; 11.33.

For what he guessed must have been at least the tenth time that morning, Marc Price pulled himself up out of the water and scrambled on to his windsurfing board. He grabbed hold of the uphaul rope, to help him keep his balance as he knelt on the board and then shakily stood up. As he did so, he tugged on the rig, slowly raising it and its sail out of the water. Remembering what he had been taught – *keep your head up, hold your arms straight, don't do things too quickly* – he pulled on the uphaul rope, hand over hand, drawing up the sail until it was almost at a ninety degree angle.

He grinned. It looked like he'd finally done it! He gave one final heave on the rope, whooped with triumph, and the rig reached ninety degrees . . . one hundred and twenty, and thirty, and forty . . . one hundred and eighty – and Marc landed with an excruciatingly embarrassing *splash!* in the water, the sail on top of him.

Marc came up for air, splattering and spluttering, until he could stagger to his feet in the shallows. As he did so, he looked ruefully at the beach, where a man dressed in a similar, brightly coloured wet suit and boots was splashing through the water towards him.

In terms of appearance the newcomer seemed the exact opposite of Marc: muscular, where Marc was strong and wiry; dark floppy hair which cascaded down his back, whereas Marc's was fashionably short and spiky and bleached blonde; a dark brooding look which made him seem older than his years, while there was always a mischievous glint in Marc's fifteen-year-old eyes. Marc looked ruefully at the newcomer.

'Guess I've just gone and made myself look like a prize idiot again, huh, Hal?' he said. 'Looks like

I'll never be champion windsurfing material like those other guys out in the bay.'

'Sure you will,' Hal promised, resisting a smile. 'This is only your first day, after all. You've got to take things one step at a time before you can windsurf.'

'I'd settle for just being able to stand up for more than a couple of seconds without going head-over-heels,' Marc replied. He looked enviously at the other windsurfers in the bay, skipping over the water with ease, and riding the currents and crosswinds like they were born to it. 'How long did it take you to learn?'

There was a sudden faraway look in Hal's eyes, which, Marc noticed for the first time, were as green as the sea. 'I can't remember a time when I didn't surf or swim,' he told him. 'My family have always lived near the sea. To me it's as natural as walking.'

'And where is home?' Marc asked pleasantly, as Hal helped him carry his board up to the beach. Holiday-makers were everywhere, sunning themselves on the sand, or queuing up to hire wind-surfing boards or to take a ride around the bay in one of the three speedboats owned by Blaise.

'A long way away,' Hal said, not wishing to commit himself – especially to someone he'd met only yesterday, when Marc had casually turned up at the beach asking for lessons. As they climbed up the beach, Marc waved to the girl who was waiting for them there: a tall, dark-haired girl dressed in a one-piece bathing suit. She smiled when she saw them and put down the book she was reading.

Marc looked at the title of the book: *Legends of King Arthur and the Knights of the Round Table*. 'You as well, Kim?' he said.

'What do you mean?' she asked, as she threw Marc and Hal towels to dry their hair.

Marc had bumped into Kim in the village shop three days ago. (It had been her who'd told him that she knew someone who was giving wind-surfing lessons down at Arthur's Bay.) She hadn't struck him as the sort of girl to believe in all the old legends. She seemed just as down-to-earth and practical as Rebecca, he'd decided, sadly.

'I wouldn't have thought you'd be the sort of person to come to Penwyn-Mar to track down the old legends,' he said.

'I'm not,' Kim retorted, sounding as if she was most put-out that Marc could even countenance such an idea. 'They're beautiful stories, but nothing more.'

'Somehow I don't think Marc quite believes that,' Hal said, wickedly. 'I suspect he secretly wants the tales of King Arthur and the Holy Grail to be true.'

'Hey, c'mon you two, stop ganging up on me!' Marc protested, but couldn't resist a smile. 'You'll find lots of locals around here who believe in the old stories of the ghost village of Penwyn-Mar, or of the water-demons.'

'Water-demons?' asked Hal, suddenly very interested.

'Sure, silkies, or whatever they call them down

here in Cornwall,' Marc said. 'Fishes in the sea –
men on dry land.'

Hal laughed. 'And you believe all those stories?'
he asked disparagingly. 'I thought that you went to
one of the top science-specialised schools in the
country.'

'Well, yes,' Marc said, thankful that none of his
teachers at the Institute were here to listen to him
now. 'But they are good stories, aren't they?'

'That's all they are: stories,' Kim repeated and
then drew their attention out to sea. Far off, away
from the windsurfers and the speedboats, and near
the Pendragon Rock lighthouse, streaks of black-
and-white were cutting a path through the waves,
effortlessly avoiding the needle-sharp rocks upon
which so many boats had foundered down through
the years. The breeze brought with it a curious,
haunting melody of whistles and calls: the lullaby
of the masters of the deep. Out there in the English
Channel, the whales were on the move.

'Now if you ask me, those are the *real* ghosts of
Penwyn-Mar,' Kim said sadly.

'The whales?' Marc asked, and watched as the
mammals glided effortlessly through the waves.

'*Orca orcinus*,' Kim explained. 'The killer whale.'

'Killer whales?' asked Hal as he watched the
whales leap and dive in the waters of the English
Channel. 'You mean, like in *Free Willy*?'

Kim smiled. 'Yes, just like in *Free Willy*,' she replied.

'But they're not really killers at all,' said Marc,
who had studied the creatures in zoology lessons

back at the Institute. 'Along with their cousins, the dolphins, they're some of the gentlest creatures alive. The only instances of them ever killing or harming humans have been when they've been provoked or when they're protecting members of their pod, or family group.'

'They're also some of the most intelligent animals on the face of the planet,' Kim said enthusiastically, as she warmed to her favourite subject.

'More intelligent than humans?' asked Hal.

'*Some* humans,' she replied mischievously and looked at Marc and at Hal in turn. 'There have been hundreds of recorded instances of them helping out people in distress: saving them from shipwrecks, that sort of thing. And look at the way they're navigating their route, avoiding all those rocks out at sea. I'd like to see a human sailor do that with such effortless grace and speed.'

'You called them "the real ghosts of Penwyn-Mar",' Marc reminded her, and he watched as the whales vanished out of sight behind Pendragon Rock. 'What did you mean?'

'I'm an oceanography and zoology student,' she told him, 'and whales are one of my specialities. I'm researching them for my University thesis. That's why I'm here at Penwyn-Mar.'

'And I thought it was just for the waves,' cracked Hal. They started to move away from the beach and up towards The Excalibur Express, a ramshackle café – and yet another of Blaise's get-rich-quick schemes.

Marc urged Kim to continue.

'They've been behaving erratically ever since I arrived here,' she told them. 'As if something is troubling them. There have been a couple of times when I've hired a speedboat from Blaise to study them more closely, and they've actually tried to attack and overturn the boat.'

'I thought you said they weren't hostile to humans,' Hal recalled.

'I did. And they're not,' came back Kim's sombre reply. 'But something's freaked them out. I found two of them washed up on the shore the other day . . .'

'Dead?' asked Marc, and Kim nodded sadly. Marc instantly started to think about what could have possibly killed the two whales. 'There was an oil tanker disaster round these parts some years ago. I remember reading about its environmental consequences in *New Scientist*. Could that have anything to do with it?'

'No,' Kim replied. 'I managed to arrange for the transportation of one of them to Penzance, where I ran some tests on it. There was no trace of disease either, when I dissected the whale and cut it open.'

'Let's change the subject, shall we?' Hal asked urgently. 'All this talk about cutting things up is making me feel queasy.'

'Sure,' said Kim. 'But there was one thing which really worried me when I was examining the dead whale . . .'

'What?' Marc sensed it was something serious.

He recognised the look in Kim's eyes. It was the same hard and determined look he'd seen time and time again in Rebecca's eyes when she was faced with a physics or a maths problem that she couldn't quite solve.

'Of course, I could have been mistaken.' Despite her words it was quite clear that Kim knew that she hadn't been mistaken at all.

'What did you discover?' Marc asked, desperate to know, while Hal displayed an uncharacteristic lack of interest.

'From its external appearance the whale was about ten years old,' she said.

'Almost middle-aged then,' Marc jibed, and then continued: 'wait a minute. You said, *external* appearance . . .'

'That's right,' Kim said, and now there was no doubting the concern in her voice. 'But when I cut it open and examined its internal organs, they were the heart and liver and lungs of a much younger animal. Two years at the very most. I just hope I'm wrong . . .'

'What are you trying to say?' Hal asked Kim, but it was Marc who answered. 'It's obvious, isn't it? What Kim is trying to say is that all the laws of nature have just been broken!'

THE PSYCHIC ZONE

2

The Watcher on the Shore

Dateline: Caer Cliffs, Penwyn-Mar;
Tuesday 25 August; 13.32.

While Marc, Kim and Hal were discussing the mystery of the whales, Rebecca and Colette had finally reached the archaeological dig. It was located some two or three miles away from Arthur's Bay and the windsurfers, on a high bluff overlooking the sea.

Supposedly the site of a Fifth Century fortress, it stood in an ideal position with its superb views of the sea and the surrounding landscape. To the faraway west – way past Grail Hallows Point – could be seen the rocks of Land's End, the southernmost tip of the Isles of Britain. To the north, the village of Penwyn-Mar, and beyond, the rocky and brutally rugged landscape of Cornwall.

Much closer to the south and south-west was

Arthur's Bay, its windsurfers tiny dots of moving colour at this distance, and the Pendragon Rock lighthouse, the scene of those mysterious lights Rebecca and Colette had spotted on their very first night in Cornwall.

Some twenty metres below Rebecca and Colette there was a tiny bay, cut off from the rest of the coast by high, nearly unscaleable rocks. Unlike its larger neighbour to the west, Balan's Bay hadn't yet been discovered by tourists – which was just as well. On her regular summer holidays here, Colette's Aunt Annie had always banned her from playing anywhere near the bay. There were quick-sands there, she had told her, ready to trap and swallow up the unsuspecting. Colette had never believed her until two hapless tourists had lost their lives there. Now the place was cordoned off from the rest of the beach by barbed-wire fencing.

A little way out to sea there stood a rocky crag of a small island, constantly being buffeted by the waves. None of the locals had set foot on Lyonesse island for years now, and disappointed tourists were informed that the place was now a private island, had been for two years, and was strictly off-bounds to everyone.

Not that Rebecca and Colette were concerned about the events of the immediate past. For the moment, Rebecca (at least) was interested in events which had taken place over fifteen centuries ago. She looked over to the main site of the dig: an area of broken walls and stones, each sectioned off by pegs and string into small three metre by three metre squares. Young people – little more than a few years older than her, and probably students – were on their hands and knees, gently picking at the ground with trowels, unearthing the remains of the old Roman-British fort. She spotted one familiar face and waved.

Joey Williams grinned, lay his trowel on the ground, and walked over to Rebecca and Colette. Joey was a young black kid from the New York slums, with a cheeky-looking face and an even cheekier manner. With his baggy jeans, up-to-the-minute trainers and streetwise clothes (the latest being a T-shirt emblazoned with the name of today's hippest fashion designer), he didn't look like the brilliant maths student he really was. Joey hated having to conform, and often looked despairingly at Rebecca's usual outfit of black jeans and top. Joey liked it like that: presenting one image, and keeping another one a secret only to be known to the chosen few. There were also other things about himself which Joey preferred most people not to know about . . .

'*Yo*, gang,' he said, and gave each of them five. Rebecca winced at his use of slang, but slapped his hand anyway.

'How are you, Joey?' she asked. 'We haven't seen much of you since we got down here to Cornwall. Except for meal-times, of course.'

'We did all agree to come on this holiday *together*,' Colette reminded Joey a little pointedly. At first, she'd never been sure how to react to him but now she was finding that she liked him a lot.

Joey shifted awkwardly from foot to foot and Rebecca and Colette both knew that they'd hit on a sore point. Joey was a loyal friend – when he got to know you, that was – and there must have been something really important to have kept him away from Marc, Rebecca and Colette for much of their vacation.

'But, guys, like this dig is one of the most sensational finds since . . . since . . .' Joey searched around in his mind for a suitable comparison, couldn't find one, and settled for: 'since Michael Jackson discovered plastic surgery.'

'Joey, it's just the remains of a Fifth Century fort, that's all,' she said, although she was excited by the find as well – if not for quite the same reasons as Joey. 'They're two-a-penny in this part of the country.'

'It's what we call *history*, Joey,' Colette said cattily. 'Although as an American you probably wouldn't know what that is.'

'Hey!' Rebecca said, trying to sound offended. 'Don't forget that I come from the States as well.'

'No you don't,' Colette grinned, enjoying the joke. 'You're far too sensible and level-headed to be a real American!'

'Thank you – I think,' Rebecca said, not altogether sure whether she'd just been complimented or not.

Joey looked disheartened, but rallied to his own

defence. 'So if this dig's so unimportant and "two-a-penny", how come this Rune guy's letting Elenore and her lot on to his land?'

'Rune? Elenore?' The names meant nothing to Rebecca and she asked Joey to explain further.

'Elenore Morgan, she's the head of the dig. You've probably seen her down in the village. About twenty-six, I'd guess. Really sassy chick, y'know – for a limey anyway,' he added as an answer to Colette's earlier good-natured insult. 'Heck, you'd never know that she was a Cambridge professor and all that. I mean, she's real sexy in a weird twenty-something sort of way . . .' Joey's face fell as Rebecca and Colette's chuckles told him that he'd just given far too much away.

'Aha!' Rebecca declared in a superior tone of voice. 'That's why you're so interested in the dig. And there were we, thinking that you'd suddenly developed an interest in archaeology!'

'When all the time you want to be this Elenore's toy-boy,' Colette said, and then wagged an admonishing finger in Joey's direction. '*Puh-lease*, Joey, she's almost old enough to be your mother!'

Joey coloured with embarrassment, realising that he'd been found out. But what the hell? Whatever else the girls might say there was clearly no getting away from the fact: Elenore Morgan was one hell of a classy broad!

'You've both of you got your wires crossed,' he claimed.

'So why is this dig just so sensational, as you call

it,' Colette said, defying her friend to prove her wrong.

Joey rammed his hands into his pockets and fixed Colette with an equally defiant stare. 'Wouldn't you say that finding King Arthur's castle was just a little bit sensational?' he asked, and was gratified when Colette let out a long whistle of appreciation.

'They've found *King Arthur's castle*?' she asked, scarcely able to believe her ears. If Joey was right then this really was a major archaeological find. Up to now, the castle at nearby Tintagel had been reputed to be King Arthur's birthplace, even though, if Colette had bothered to check the facts (which she rarely did), she would have discovered that the ruin there had really been built by the Normans.

'Did I say that?' asked Joey, all coy now that Colette's interest had been aroused, and also enormously proud of the way he had managed to turn around the subject of the conversation so expertly.

Rebecca looked cynically at Joey. She knew him much better than Colette, having spent much more time with him at school, and she realised how smoothly he'd changed the subject of his infatuation with the apparently pretty leader of the archaeological dig.

'What Joey should have said is that Elenore Morgan and her team have uncovered a Fifth Century Roman fort, which probably belonged to a great Anglo-Saxon war chief,' she corrected them.

'Well, wasn't Arthur around in the Fifth Century?' Joey asked, a little ruefully. That was the trouble with Rebecca, he reflected: she always liked to ruin a perfectly good story.

'*An* Anglo-Saxon war chief was around in the Fifth Century, beating off the last of the Roman invaders,' Rebecca conceded. 'And yes, his name probably was *Arturius*.'

'So I'm right,' Joey said, but typically, Rebecca hadn't finished yet.

'But there's no evidence that he came from around here, or even that he was a king,' she continued. 'The first reference to him was as *dux bellorum*.'

'*Dux* what?' Colette asked.

'*Dux bellorum*,' Rebecca repeated knowledgeably. 'It's Latin for war chief. He was the real Arthur.'

'That's right,' a voice said, and Rebecca, Colette and Joey turned around to see a blonde-haired woman in her mid-twenties approach them. Even the sloppy army-surplus dungarees she was wearing couldn't disguise the fact that she was a very attractive woman indeed. This had to be Elenore Morgan, the head of the dig, Rebecca realised.

'Arthur was a war chief, nothing more and nothing less,' Elenore said, after Joey had introduced her to Rebecca and Colette. 'And all the legends of Merlin and the Round Table and the Holy Grail grew up around him, just as they would do around any great and charismatic figure. I imagine in time the same thing will happen with your Princess Diana.'

'*Our* Princess Diana?' Colette asked. 'You're not English then. Where do you come from?'

Elenore frowned and there was a curious expression on her face. Colette, who was more sensitive to such things than the others, thought it was a look of pain, but then Elenore smiled and it passed.

'A long way from here,' she said, her voice not betraying the emotion that Colette was sure had been there. Elenore led them back to the dig.

'But this place could be King Arthur's castle, right?' Joey asked, determined that Elenore should lend at least some credibility to his story.

'As far as we know it's only the site of a war chief's fort,' Elenore said, and Rebecca shot Joey a look which said *I told you so*. 'But Broderick Rune seems to think otherwise.'

'Broderick Rune?' asked Rebecca. The name sounded dark and ponderous, and full of hidden menace. 'Who's he?'

'The man who's funding the dig,' Elenore said, and then looked nervously around, as if to see if anyone was listening. 'A thoroughly nasty piece of work, if you ask me. He owns the island down there in Balan's Bay.'

Rebecca looked over to the rocky crag and then turned back to Elenore. 'If he's a nasty piece of work like you say, then why are you working for him?'

'When a multi-billionaire decides to pump money into a survey of what he thinks might be somehow connected with King Arthur, and *I know* is probably a significant Fifth Century site, then you tend to put your personal prejudices aside,' Elenore said. She looked away from the site and towards the sea. 'But if you want to know the truth, I'm secretly glad I came to Penwyn-Mar. It's strange but when I arrived here it felt like I was coming home . . .'

'But you said that you came from a long way from here,' Colette said, and now there was no mistaking the sadness in Elenore's voice.

'Yes, I did, didn't I?' Elenore said, and looked at her watch. She sighed. 'I guess we'll call it a day on the site.'

'This early?' Rebecca asked.

Elenore glanced over at the other workers on the site. 'I'm sure they'd like to get in a spot of wind-surfing,' she said. 'Besides, we've found nothing today. Not a piece of broken pottery, not a single coin, just one big zero. We could all do with a rest. Perhaps we'll be luckier tomorrow.'

'Maybe you're just not looking in the right places,' Joey said, with a twinkle in his eye. 'And maybe you need some extra-special help!'

Rebecca and Colette exchanged knowing looks, but Elenore asked Joey what he meant.

'Just trust yourself to Joseph Williams, ma'am,' Joey announced grandly, and affected the sort of courtly bow he'd seen on *Masterpiece Theatre* back home in the States.

'What's he doing?' Elenore asked the two girls, as they all watched Joey stride over to the dig and ask the other workers there to give him space.

'Joey has certain... talents,' Rebecca said mysteriously.

'He's sort of like one of those metal detectors you see people using on the beach sometimes,' Colette said with a grin: 'only with a worse attitude. Just watch.'

Joey had now closed his eyes and was standing in the middle of the cleared dig, arms outstretched in front of him and a look of intent concentration on his face. A casual observer would have said that he was listening out for something. But what Joey heard was not the sound of the waves on the beach below, or the cries of the seagulls, or even the hushed whispers of the onlookers. Joey was listening to the sounds of the planet itself, tuning in on the electromagnetic vibrations of the very earth.

Slowly, Joey started to move, eyes still closed, like a sleep-walker. He walked over to the very edge of the site and then opened his eyes. He pointed to the ground.

'Dig there,' he said.

'Don't be ridiculous, Joey,' Elenore said. 'That's way past the outer wall of the fort. You'll find nothing there.'

'Dig there.' Joey was adamant.

'I'd do as he says,' Rebecca said. 'I didn't believe it at first, but trust me, he knows what he's talking about.'

Elenore shrugged her shoulders, but nevertheless asked one of her colleagues to dig in the
spot Joey had indicated. Within minutes, he had
managed to uncover a finely-fashioned drinking
cup.

'I don't believe it,' Elenore said, as she held the
object up to the light. 'This is a perfect example of
late Roman-British pottery.'

'Looks like a pretty cool cup to me,' Joey
quipped, his chest swelling with pride. 'Just the
right size for a nice Doctor Pepper.'

'How did you do that?' Elenore asked, after she
had handed the cup to one of her assistants for safe-
keeping.

'Just a knack I have,' Joey said nonchalantly.
'You've either got it or you haven't!'

'It's just like dowsing,' Rebecca explained. 'Joey
can tune into the electromagnetic pulses in the
earth.'

'And *voilà!* Your Anglo-Saxon cup,' Joey said.
'Maybe they should send me to Texas and get me
to drill for oil.'

'He's great for finding lost socks,' Colette said,
refusing to show just how impressed she really was
by Joey's abilities. In fact, she was more than a little
jealous. She too possessed some psychic abilities,
but none as strong or as precise as Joey's.

'You name it, Elenore, and I'll find it for you!'
Joey said, and waved his arms around in an
expansive gesture. As he did so, he was unaware
that they were being watched. A tall man, immacu-

lately dressed in a stylish black suit and wearing dark glasses, was watching them from the edge of the dig. He took a mobile phone from out of his pocket and dialled a number. He had seen everything and he now knew that it was vital his master should know what he had learnt.

Elenore smiled, putting her arm over Joey's shoulder, and the young boy blushed. 'Joey, you and I are going to make a great team!' she announced. 'With your abilities and my archaeological experience, we could make some fantastic discoveries!'

And Elenore Morgan was absolutely right – but in a way neither she nor Joey, Rebecca nor Colette, could ever have guessed.

Dateline: Tristam Cottage, Penwyn-Mar; Tuesday 28 August; 21.18.

'She must be wrong,' Rebecca said later that evening when she, Joey and Colette had met back up with Marc at the cottage belonging to Colette's Aunt Annie. 'It's absolutely impossible for a ten-year-old whale to have the internal organs of a much younger animal.'

'A little while back you'd've said that it was impossible for a person to read minds, or to sense the presence of Roman pottery in the ground,' Marc said reasonably.

'But now I've *seen* Joey do both those things,'

Rebecca countered. 'I'm a scientist, Marc, and I believe only the evidence of my own eyes. Just as you should, in fact.'

'But without imagination many of the great scientific advances of the century might not have been made,' Marc riposted. 'Calm and detached scientific thinking is all very well, but sometimes you need some open-minded lunatics like me to help you along the way.'

It was a familiar argument, one which Marc and Rebecca had had many times in the past, and Joey told them so.

'Look, you guys, cut it out, will you? Who cares about whales with dodgy insides, or why the people of Penwyn-Mar look much younger than they ought to? There're more important things to worry about.'

'That's not like you, Joey,' Marc said. 'Normally you're the first of us to poke his nose in where it's not wanted.'

'That's because our Joey's in *lurrve*!' Colette crowed, and received a friendly punch in the ribs from Joey for her remarks.

Just then Annie Russell entered the room. This was probably just as well, as there was a distinct danger of open warfare breaking out between Joey and Colette, with the sofa cushions being the weapons, and her cut-glass collection on the sideboard the immediate casualties.

Annie was a tall and graceful blonde whose youthful good looks belied her forty-nine years. As

Rebecca had said, she looked much younger. However, the stern look she gave Colette and Joey as she walked in, showed every bit of her age.

'Someone came for you while you were out,' she told Joey.

'Elenore?' he asked hopefully, and Colette stifled a giggle. Annie shook her head, and Joey frowned. Apart from Elenore, he knew nobody else in Penwyn-Mar.

'He wouldn't give his name,' Annie said, in response to Joey's question, 'but he said he'd come back. He was an outsider,' she when on, 'someone I don't know. Tall, with dark glasses, and an attitude about him. One of Broderick Rune's men, from the look of him.'

'Broderick Rune?' Rebecca asked. 'What would a billionaire want with Joey?'

'Whatever it is, I'd have no part in it if I were you, Joey,' Annie told him.

'You don't like him then?' Rebecca said and remembered what Elenore had said about the billionaire: *a thoroughly nasty piece of work, if you ask me.*

'He's brought nothing but trouble since he came to Penwyn-Mar two years ago,' Annie said. 'There used to be a marina on that small island off the coast. It brought in valuable tourist revenue. But he closed it down when he bought the island.'

'Blaise is still making a packet out of the Arthurian legends, and hiring out speedboats and windsurfing boards,' Marc pointed out.

'Rune would like to put a stop to that as well,' Annie continued. 'He probably thinks the wind-surfers bring down the tone of the village. Although why a man like him should care about a village like Penwyn-Mar is beyond me.'

'What do you mean?' Colette was curious. Her aunt was usually the most tolerant of women. For her to speak like this of the mysterious Broderick Rune must mean that he was seriously bad news.

'Think of it,' she said. 'The man is a billionaire several times over. From what I hear he made his fortune designing software programs for the US military.'

'Gross,' was Joey's comment, and the others nodded in agreement.

'So why should a man like him come to a sleepy village, whose only attractions are its legends of King Arthur and the surf around Arthur's Bay?'

'I take your point,' Marc said. 'I suppose it's a bit like Bill Gates giving it all up for a poky little semi in Preston.'

'Maybe he's just a rich nutter who wants to get away from it all,' Rebecca suggested. As far as she was concerned Broderick Rune could do whatever he wanted. And with his money, he probably would.

'Perhaps,' was Annie's guarded comment. 'So stay away from him, Joey. If you know what's good for you, that is.'

Dateline: Tristam Cottage;
Wednesday 26 August; 00.37.

Colette tossed and turned in bed, but still she couldn't get to sleep. Through her open window she could hear the whales calling far out at sea. It was a familiar enough sound to her, one which she usually found very comforting every time she came to Cornwall. Their calls, and the gentle lapping of the sea on the shingles of the beach directly outside Tristam Cottage, normally meant that she fell asleep as soon as her head hit the pillow.

But not tonight. The whales sounded different somehow, and Colette wished she could understand the song they were singing. Joey would know, she thought, and briefly considered tip-toeing next door to the room which he was sharing with Marc. There seemed to be an overbearing sadness in the whales' song, a terrible keening which made it impossible for her to fall asleep.

She glanced over to the bed in which Rebecca was sleeping soundly. She didn't seem to be affected by the whales' song at all.

Realising that she wouldn't get to sleep now, Colette got out of bed, threw her dressing gown over her shoulders, and walked to the window. She looked out over the sand to the sea's edge. To the right she could see the old boathouse in which Blaise locked his motorboats and windsurfing boards for the night. And standing by the old boathouse with her back to Colette, was Elenore Morgan.

She was motionless, not even moving as the wind blew her long hair in her face, or as the waves lapped and covered her bare feet, and soaked the bottoms of her jeans. She seemed mesmerised, but by what, Colette wondered. By the whales, singing in the distance? By the sea itself? Or something much more sinister?

'Elenore!' Colette called out. 'Elenore, are you all right?'

No reply. Just the waves rushing to shore and the whales singing their mournful song.

'Elenore!' Colette tried once again, but still Elenore didn't acknowledge her. She was like a statue, still and cold and unresponsive.

And then something seemed to snap in Elenore. She started to cry, doubling up in her anguish. Her sobs drowned out even the whales' song coming in across the waves.

'Who am I?' she cried out in her pain. 'What have I done? Why have I come back here?'

Colette rushed out of her bedroom not bothering to wake Rebecca, down the stairs, out of Tristam Cottage, and on to the beach and down to the sea. But when she reached the water's edge, Elenore was nowhere to be seen. Had she imagined seeing her there?

Colette clutched her dressing gown closer to her body. For some reason she felt very, very cold. She looked up and down the beach. No sign of Elenore, no evidence that she had ever been on the beach.

'Elenore, are you there? Are you all right? Where are you? You don't have to worry. It's only me. It's only Colette.'

There was, of course, no reply; just the mocking sound of the waves. Even the whales seemed to have stopped their singing now. Colette was alone on the beach.

Or not quite alone. She looked up into the night sky and saw green lights flickering and dazzling in the air. There was no mistaking it this time. These lights weren't some atmospheric disturbance, as Rebecca had suggested. Nor were they any kind of natural phenomenon – at least none that Colette had heard of.

Evil. Unnatural. Alien. Yes, *alien*! That was what these lights were.

Suddenly Colette felt very, very afraid. She remembered some of the tales from her childhood that Blaise used to tell her; of the water-demons which lurked beneath the waves, ready to drag down the unwary swimmer; of demons in the shape of men but with the hearts of devils; of the lost village of Penwyn-Mar and its ghosts.

Now it was Colette's turn to be mesmerised as she stared out to sea. Something was swimming through the water towards her. At first she thought that it was an orca, for the approaching creature certainly moved as swiftly and as gracefully as the whales. And then she realised that the whales had gone and that she was left alone; alone and defenceless with this new creature from the depths of the sea. With the creature that, for all she knew, had already taken Elenore and was now coming for her.

Colette tried to run: she found she couldn't. She tried to cry out for help: no sound came from her lips. The lights in the sky seemed to glow even more brightly. From somewhere far off she heard a distant rumbling, like the threat of approaching thunder.

The creature had almost reached the beach now. It pulled itself out of the water, and started to plod across the sands towards her. There was no place to run now; no way she could escape this creature from the deep.

The creature reached out its hand to Colette . . .

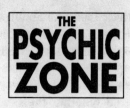

THE PSYCHIC ZONE

3

Footprints in the Sand

Dateline: The beach at Penwyn-Mar;
Wednesday 26 August; 00.46

'Are you all right?' the figure from out of the waves asked her, and Colette mentally kicked herself. She felt such an idiot! The creature she had imagined to be a water-demon, or some other such nonsense, was nothing more than a long-haired swimmer in his mid-twenties, wearing Speedos. He also looked vaguely familiar.

'My name's Hal,' he said. 'I'm sorry if I startled you.' Again, he offered her his hand to shake. Colette took it, and then frowned. Hal's touch felt cold and clammy; the sea must be colder than it looked.

'I thought –' Colette began and then stopped herself: 'forget what I thought. It doesn't matter.'

'I was out there having a swim, near the light-house, when I saw you standing here,' Hal said, and walked over to a rock where he had stashed away a towel and a pair of sneakers. He hurriedly put the shoes on and then started to dry his tousled hair. 'I wondered whether there was something wrong.'

'Swimming? At this time?' Was she being overly suspicious, or was there something in Hal's explanation which didn't quite ring true?

'Sure,' he said. 'It's the only chance I get. During the day I've got my hands full teaching the tourists how to windsurf.'

Colette finally realised who Hal was, and dismissed any suspicions she might have entertained about him. 'Of course! You're the guy who's teaching my friend, Marc,' she said and then asked, 'tell me, is he really as hopeless at it as he looks?'

Hal laughed and dropped his voice to a confidential whisper. 'Not as good as some,' he admitted, 'but not as bad as others. He'll get the knack any day now. Now, you didn't answer my question. What were you doing standing there looking out to sea?'

'It wasn't me,' Colette said, and wondered whether she should tell Hal that it had been Elenore that he had seen. Finally she decided not to. After all, Elenore might not want a complete stranger to know that she had been spotted crying. 'I thought I saw someone too and came down to look. But when I arrived here, she – I mean, *they* – had gone.'

'Probably someone on their way home from The Smugglers' Retreat then,' Hal guessed, and struggled into a pair of old jeans which he'd also hidden behind the rock. Colette chuckled at his awkward attempts to get into them.

'It'd help if you hadn't put your shoes on first,' she pointed out.

Hal looked sheepishly at her with those large sea-green eyes of his. *He is rather cute*, Colette thought and prayed that Joey would never find out. He'd tease her as mercilessly as she had him earlier that evening. He tugged at the jeans, and finally pulled them up and over his trainers. 'All the seawater's probably gone to my head,' he said and laughed as he fastened the jeans over his Speedos.

'Did you hear the whales earlier?' Colette asked. 'That was what kept me awake.'

'Yes, I did,' Hal said, a little sadly, Colette thought. 'They're fine now, though.'

Suddenly there was the muffled sound of an explosion from somewhere near the lighthouse at Pendragon Rock, which was rapidly followed by another and then another. Colette instinctively grabbed Hal's arm. 'Listen! Aren't those explosions?' she asked urgently.

Hal frowned and for a moment didn't say anything. 'It sounded like the waves crashing on to the rocks,' he said, not particularly convincingly. 'It's nothing to worry about.'

Colette looked strangely at Hal. She didn't have

to be even mildly psychic to know that the wind-surfer was lying.

'You shouldn't have been swimming near Pendragon Rock,' she reproved him, as he started to move up the beach and she followed him. 'The rocks there are dangerous. Even the locals avoid them.'

'You don't see the whales hurting themselves do you?' he said with a smile.

'But you're not a whale, are you?'

'Of course not! But I am a good swimmer,' he told her. 'Now, are you sure that you're OK?'

'I'm fine,' Colette reassured him.

'Then I'll say goodbye,' Hal said, and shook her by the hand – once again, Colette felt his cold and clammy touch – before walking off into the distance.

Colette watched him go and the trail of foot-prints he left behind him in the sand. And then she spotted a third set of footprints. These weren't bare-footed footprints, like hers; nor were they the prints left by Hal's trainers.

The third set of prints had been made by a two-legged creature who walked with webbed feet. A creature the size of a man . . .

Dateline: Caer Cliffs;
Wednesday 26 August; 09.47.

Rebecca, Colette and Joey had turned up at the dig following an early-morning phone-call from Elenore. They'd started digging in the place Joey had indicated the previous day, she'd told them, and already they'd come up with some priceless objects: ancient artefacts from the last days of the Roman occupation of Britain. Could Joey help them out further, Elenore had asked, by 'zapping' out some more buried relics?

'Just you try and stop me!' Joey had said, after he'd put the phone down in Tristam Cottage. He'd rubbed his hands together in anticipation and had then asked Marc if he'd any 'really cool, but not so cool that she thinks I really give a damn' aftershave.

'Joey, you don't honestly think that you have a chance with Elenore. She's almost fifteen years older than you!' Rebecca had asked reasonably.

'You never know, she might need a friend,' Colette had said, and both Rebecca and Joey had expressed amazement at her change of view. 'She might be lonely.'

'And what makes you think that?' Rebecca had asked.

'Just a hunch,' Colette had said, having decided to keep her midnight trip to the beach to herself.

When they arrived at the dig however, Colette managed to have a quiet word with Elenore, before

Joey 'did his stuff', as Elenore called it.

'How are you feeling today?' Colette asked and Elenore had fixed her with a baffled stare.

'I'm fine,' she said. 'Why shouldn't I be?'

'It's just that I saw you down on the beach last night, and I wondered if you might be upset about something.'

'Colette, you must have been mistaken. I was fast asleep all last night,' Elenore claimed. 'You can't have spotted me down on the beach.'

But I did, I know I did, Colette thought, but outwardly she agreed that, yes, she must have been mistaken after all.

Elenore quickly changed the subject and turned to Joey. 'OK, Joey, are you ready to do the biz?' she asked.

'Ready?' Joey asked in amazement. 'Ready? Lady, I was born ready! Where do you want me to start?'

Elenore indicated a spot away from the main part of the dig. 'We suspect the foundations of the fort might stretch way over there,' she said. 'But we don't have the time to excavate there unless we're certain.'

'So you want me to find out if it's going to be worth your while?' Joey asked. 'Don't worry, Elenore, it's gonna be a cinch!'

As Joey started to move towards the spot, Rebecca noticed a black-suited man in dark glasses looking at them from afar.

'Who's the creep in the dark glasses?' she asked,

wondering if he was the same person who had called for Joey the previous day: the one Annie had instinctively mistrusted.

'Malvaine,' Elenore replied. 'He's one of Broderick Rune's men.'

'So what's he doing here?' Rebecca asked. 'He doesn't seem to me to be the kind of person who's into archaeology. Torturing, killing and maiming, maybe, but archaeology, no.'

'He's just keeping an eye on things for his boss, that's all,' Elenore said. 'The dig is on Broderick Rune's land, after all. I guess he wants to make sure that we don't make off with any treasures we might find.'

'Don't you find it strange that Rune's so interested in the dig?' Rebecca asked. 'I wouldn't imagine a man who has made a fortune out of computer software would be interested in the past.'

'Like I say, I don't ask questions. I'm just grateful that he's financing the dig,' Elenore reminded her. 'That doesn't mean I have to like him as well.'

'Keep quiet,' Colette told them. 'Joey's doing the biz again.'

A hush descended on the dig as Joey wandered over the ground – eyes closed and arms out-stretched – trying to divine the presence of any precious artefacts that might be buried in the ground. He tried to clear his mind: emptying it of any extraneous and unnecessary thoughts; opening it up to whatever might be in the ground. waiting to be unearthed.

Nothing. He turned back to the others, and shrugged his shoulders helplessly. 'Sorry, guys. Zilch,' he said. 'One big zero. Maybe the other time was just a fluke.'

Elenore looked disappointed and suggested that he try another spot, closer to the edge of the cliff. Joey looked equally disappointed.

'Hey, whadya want me to do? Fall off the cliff? A guy could get seriously killed walking around there with his eyes shut!'

Elenore grinned. 'Don't worry, Joey, I'll hold your hand so that you won't fall.'

'Now that's more like it!' Joey said, and held out his hand for Elenore to take. Rebecca and Colette exchanged a look which seemed to say: *Men! What are they like!*

With his hand in Elenore's, Joey started to explore the edge of the cliff, while Rebecca, Colette and the others workers on the dig-site looked on. Malvaine watched Joey as well, and once again took out his mobile and punched out a number on its pad.

Joey walked up and down the cliff edge for several minutes while the others waited with bated breath. Finally he gave up.

'Sorry, Elenore, I can't –' he began and then stiffened. He grabbed Elenore's hand tightly, so tightly that she winced in pain. 'Wait a minute! There is something! I can feel it. It's right under-neath us.'

'What is it, Joey?' asked Colette, who ran up to

them, followed by Rebecca. 'What is it that you can feel?'

Joey screwed up his eyes in concentration, and his brow furrowed with the effort of channelling his thoughts into the ground. 'I . . . I don't know . . .' he said through gritted teeth. 'It's hard . . . cold . . .'

Elenore looked at her other site workers. 'Could it be a sword or some sort of weapon?' she asked them. This was the site of an old Fifth Century fort, after all.

'A *sword*,' repeated Colette and looked at Rebecca. 'You don't think . . . ?'

'No, I don't! Rebecca snapped back, even though she was equally as excited by whatever it was that Joey had detected buried deep in the earth. 'Excalibur is just a myth, like the Round Table and the Holy Grail.'

'Well, don't just stand there,' Elenore said to her fellow workers. 'Everybody get digging!'

They started digging in the place Joey had indicated, with even Rebecca and Colette lending a hand. But Malvaine continued his silent watch, only occasionally breaking it to mutter something into his mobile.

After a good half-hour or so of concentrated digging, Elenore and her team had created quite a large hole. She stood up, put down her shovel and clapped her hands together in a business-like gesture.

'OK, guys, that's the heavy work out of the way,'

she said, and a muttered cheer came up from the crowd of diggers.

'Trust Marc to be down on the beach when there's really hard work to do,' Rebecca said wryly, and rested on her own shovel. In the far-off distance she could see the windsurfers in Arthur's Bay.

'Get your trowels out now,' Elenore instructed. 'And remember, go carefully. We don't know what's down there underneath the soil. If it's more pottery then we don't want to smash it, do we?'

Rebecca, Joey and Colette joined the others on their hands and knees, and started to dig away at the loose earth. For long minutes no one said a word, as they all searched for the tell-tale glint of the metal of a sword, or a piece of broken pottery, or a coin bearing the head of some long-dead Roman emperor.

It was Colette who made the first discovery: an elaborate twisted band of metal, which shone golden in the morning sun as she gently prised it out of the ground.

'It's beautiful,' she said as she passed it over to Elenore, who took it from her with enormous care. 'What is it?'

'It's a *torc*,' she explained. 'A sort of necklace worn by British warriors.'

'So this *is* a British fort after all,' Rebecca said.

'Of course,' said Elenore, and, after handing the *torc* to one of her colleagues, continued with her digging.

Shortly afterwards, Rebecca pulled a tiny piece

of bent and buckled metal from out of the ground. She handed it triumphantly to Elenore, who examined it with interest. It was a coin, and, even though it had been worn down during the long centuries, the head on the face of the coin was just about visible.

'The Emperor Constantine,' she said finally. 'That tells us a lot.'

'It does?' Joey was none the wiser.

'Sure,' Elenore said, smiling at Joey's ignorance. 'He reigned from –' she closed her eyes briefly as she tried to remember her dates '– AD307 to AD324.'

'So that means that the site is earlier than you originally thought,' Rebecca realised.

'Yes,' Elenore replied and gave an apologetic look to Joey. 'So much for your dreams of King Arthur, Joey. Sorry.'

'No probs,' Joey said generously, even though he really would have liked the fort to have been built on the site of King Arthur's fabled Camelot. 'I'm just really impressed that you can remember all those dates and stuff.'

'I wish there were other things I could remember as well.'

'What do you mean?'

'Never mind.'

Joey frowned, wondering what was troubling Elenore, but he chose not to pursue the matter. Instead, he carried on with his digging. If Rebecca and Colette had both come up with something then he sure as heck wasn't going to be left out!

What he found just a few minutes later took his breath away. He pulled the object out of the ground and held it up for everyone to see.

'What is it?' Elenore asked as she took it from Joey and examined it. It was a small rectangle of transparent plastic, containing what seemed to her to be intricate circuitry which glinted in the light of the sun. She passed it over to Rebecca, who recognised it immediately for what it was.

'It's an integrated circuit,' she said slowly.

'A what?' asked Colette.

'A silicon chip,' Rebecca said.

'Someone must have dropped it here,' Elenore said. And then the incredible truth dawned on her, just as it had also dawned on Rebecca. Rebecca nodded her head in agreement.

'Exactly,' she said. 'Someone did drop it. Someone dropped a silicon chip here on this site – over fifteen hundred years before computers had even been invented!'

Dateline: Arthur's Bay;
Wednesday 26 August; 14.11

Hal looked on approvingly as Marc rode the waves on his board, skilfully turning the rig this way and that so the wind would catch the sail and send him skimming off in the required direction. Marc was growing in confidence, Hal realised, and it was that, plus a modicum of technique, which really counted in windsurfing.

On the beach, Colette checked her watch, wishing that she could be out there in the water with Marc instead of staying on the land. When she had come down here from the dig, Hal had made no mention of their encounter of last night, but it was clear from his off-hand manner with her that he was worried in case she mentioned it to Marc or the others.

What *had* Hal been doing that night? She certainly didn't believe his story of a midnight swim. Had he been somehow responsible for those explosions they had both heard? All she knew was that Hal wasn't quite what he seemed.

'He's quite a good-looker, isn't he?' said Kim, who had come up to join Colette and sat down on the sand beside her.

Colette giggled, enjoying the conspiratorial all-girls-together chat. 'I suppose so,' she admitted. 'Is he your boyfriend?'

Kim shook her head. 'I've my own boyfriend back at University,' she told her. 'Besides I've only got to know him since I've been at Penwyn-Mar. According to Blaise, he hasn't been here much longer than me.'

'Oh?' Colette was interested now. 'And no one knows where he comes from either?'

'Or where in Penwyn-Mar he lives, but then I gather that Blaise doesn't ask too many questions,'

Kim said, and Colette had to admit that she was right.

'I suppose that as long as he's got someone to help him with the hiring out of surfboards and as long as he can take his cut from Hal's lessons, then Blaise is happy enough,' Colette decided. 'So when did Hal arrive in the village?'

'About the same time as Elenore Morgan and her archaeologists,' she replied. 'Why do you ask?'

'No special reason,' Colette lied. 'Did you hear the whales last night?'

'Yes,' Kim said, and laughed as she watched Marc fall over in the water. Then she became serious again. 'They're unhappy. I wish I could discover why.'

'You think we can communicate with them?' Colette asked, intrigued by the possibility.

'Who's to say that they're not trying to communicate with us at this moment and we just can't speak their language?' Kim asked enigmatically. She stood up and tossed the book she was reading to the ground. 'You want to see something really impressive?'

Colette considered the matter. If it was a question of choosing between watching Marc make a fool of himself in the water while she waited for Rebecca, Joey and Elenore who were still up at the dig, or seeing 'something really impressive', she knew which one she'd pick.

She stood up and followed Kim along the beach, until they were way out of sight of Marc and Hal and the other windsurfers. Kim took her to a small rocky cove, just in the shadow of Grail Hallows Point and told Colette to stay on the beach while she walked out on to a rocky promontory which jutted out to sea.

'You asked me if we can communicate with the whales out at sea,' Kim said. 'Just you watch this.' She took out a whistle from the back pocket of her 501s, and gave three short bursts on it. She waited for a few moments and then blew again, this time producing three long whistles. Colette watched on, mystified.

'What are you doing?' she asked. Kim turned back to Colette and grinned.

'Calling a friend,' she said. 'Wait and see . . .'

Colette looked out to sea, wondering what Kim was talking about.

'This'll show you how intelligent the orcas really are,' Kim said, still looking at Colette and with her back to the sea. 'I've trained some of them to respond to individual whistles. With any luck, we're going to have a visitor any moment now.'

Colette continued to look out to sea and, sure enough, cutting through the waves and heading towards the coast, she could see the distinctive dorsal fin of a killer whale. She watched as the whale leapt into the air and then dived back into the water, in a stunning balletic display of grace and agility. She clapped her hands in delight.

'He's so beautiful,' she said, admiring the sleek yet powerful body, the black-and-white markings on its belly, and the white star-shaped patch just above its snout.

'That's old Starshine, and he's a she,' Kim laughed. She tossed the whistle over to Colette and suggested that she have a go as well. Kim still hadn't looked out to sea to greet the whale, but she was enjoying watching Colette's expression of genuine amazement.

'And you mean that she recognises that series of whistles as her very own?' Colette asked, and, when Kim nodded her head, added: 'that's amazing for a whale so young.'

'Young?' Kim asked. 'Don't be crazy, Starshine's twelve or thirteen years old if she's –' she broke off and with growing apprehension turned to look at the whale she had just summoned to the beach. She was small – obviously a very young creature – and, as she approached Kim and Colette, her movements slowly became sluggish and strained.

'It can't be!' Kim gasped as Starshine approached the shallows, and she knelt down and bent over to pat her on the snout. Starshine squeaked out a welcome, but her voice was slight and muted.

'You must be mistaken,' Colette said. She watched on in horror as Starshine started to convulse in the water.

'No.' Kim's voice was firm and certain. 'This is Starshine. I recognise the star on her head.'

'But she's so young,' Colette said, and then choked back a sob, as she watched the killer whale give a final shudder and then turn belly-up in the water.

'Yes,' said Kim, as she turned back to Colette with a grim look on her face, 'and now she's dead. So, now do you believe me about that whale back in Penzance?'

But Colette had no time to answer as she heard someone call her name. She tore her eyes away from the dead whale and saw Rebecca, Elenore, and Joey approaching them. There was a distraught look on all of their faces.

'You must come quickly,' Elenore said, and then gasped in horror at the sight of the dead whale.

'Why? What's happened?'

'It's Broderick Rune,' said Rebecca. 'He's gone and closed down the dig!'

THE PSYCHIC ZONE

4

Malvaine

Dateline: Grail Hallows Point;
Wednesday 26 August; 15.16.

'He can't just *close down* the dig,' Colette protested as soon as Rebecca had told them the news. Shortly after Colette had left them at the dig, Malvaine had apparently turned up with a bunch of men in military-style uniforms, and had moved the diggers off the land. The dig was now closed down forever, they were informed curtly, and their contracts and payments would shortly be curtailed.

'Broderick Rune is a rich man,' Elenore said bitterly. 'He can do exactly what he wants to do.'

'But why close down the dig *now*?' Colette wanted to know as she left Kim, who was still tending to the dead Starshine. 'It just doesn't make sense.'

'Oh yes, it does,' Joey said and reached into the inside pocket of his baseball jacket. He handed her the microcircuit Elenore had found.

'*This* is the reason for him closing down the dig?' she asked in amazement. It tingled in her hands – for a moment it even seemed to glow, as if somehow recognising her touch – and she hurriedly passed it over to Colette.

'It looks as though we've found something we weren't supposed to find,' Rebecca guessed.

'Or something Broderick Rune wanted us to find,' Joey said mysteriously.

'What do you mean, Joey?' Colette asked.

'Remember what Annie said,' Joey went on. 'What possible interest could a guy like Rune have in an ancient fort and a pile of broken pottery and old coins?'

Just then, Marc and Hal walked up to the beach towards them. They were both still wearing their windsurfing gear and their hair was wet and dripping. Hal took in the scene instantly. He looked curiously at Rebecca and the others – and in particular at Elenore, whom he had never met before – and then crossed over to Kim, who was silently sobbing by the water's edge, trying to come to terms with the fact that her beloved Starshine was dead.

'What's with you guys?' Marc asked cheerily, with his typical lack of tact. 'Why aren't you up at the dig, poking around in your boring old bones?'

'The dig's been closed down, that's why,' Rebecca said.

'Not from where I was standing,' Marc said.

'What are you talking about?

'I was out in Arthur's Bay windsurfing –' Marc said. 'Say, did I ever tell you that I'm getting real good at it now? Hal says he can't believe how much I've improved in just one day.'

'Marc, big buddy, give us the nitty-gritty!' Joey said, irritably.

Marc seemed put out at not being allowed the opportunity to show off but came to the point nevertheless. 'I saw some heavy-duty digging equipment being driven to the site,' he told them, and wondered why Elenore was suddenly looking so angry. 'Trucks, bulldozers, cranes: that kind of thing. It looks like this Rune guy is really serious about the dig after all.'

'The idiot!' Elenore exploded in an uncharacteristic burst of temper. 'That's a prime Fifth Century archaeological site. He'll destroy everything we've discovered. All these months of hard work for nothing!'

Hal and Kim came up to them, and there was a curious look in Hal's eyes as he looked at Elenore. Kim's own eyes were red from mourning the loss of Starshine.

'What's up?' he asked.

'That cretin Broderick Rune is what's up, Hal,' Elenore said angrily. She told Hal and Kim the full story.

'Then you'll have to stop him,' Kim said simply when Elenore had finished – glad to have something to take her mind off the whale's death.

'I intend to,' Elenore said, with fiery determination. She turned to Rebecca and Joey. 'Are you coming with me?'

'Sure we are,' Joey replied.

Marc and the others offered to accompany them, but Rebecca shook her head. They'd be much more profitably employed by going down to the village and seeing if they could raise some local opposition to Broderick Rune's action, she argued. Surely there must be some local by-law which prevented Rune from excavating the site without a licence or planning permission.

'You'll be lucky,' Hal said, as the others left. 'Judging by what I hear from Blaise, Broderick Rune's got the local council in the palm of his hand. How do you think he managed to buy his own private island, or have the old tin mines closed down, without so much as murmur of official opposition?'

'Just *try*, will you?' Elenore said, and then went off with Rebecca and Joey.

'She's one very angry woman,' Marc said after Elenore was out of earshot.

'Yes,' Hal said and nodded his head thoughtfully. 'How did she know my name, though? We've never met until just now.'

'She must have heard me mention it,' Marc suggested.

'Yes, that must be it.' But Hal didn't sound convinced. He glanced over to Colette and for the first time noticed the microcircuit in her hand. 'What's that?' he asked.

'Something we found at the dig,' she said, and handed it over to him.

Hal turned it over in his hand, examining it. '*You* found it?' his tone was suddenly urgent – hostile even.

'Well, not me exactly,' Colette admitted. 'It was Elenore herself who actually found it.'

Hal was about to quiz Colette further when Kim interrupted.

'Look can we stop worrying about microcircuits and archaeological digs for a second?' she asked and brushed a tear from her eye. 'It might just have escaped everyone's notice, but we have a dead whale back there. A dead whale who, for some reason is several years younger than she was yesterday.'

'Kim's right,' Marc agreed. 'We have to tell someone. We must find out what s killing off the whales like this.'

'Could it have something to do with the explosions we heard last night?' Colette asked.

'Explosions? What explosions?' This was news to Marc and he asked her to explain.

'It was the wind crashing against Pendragon Rock, that was all,' Hal said, after Colette had told her story.

'There were lights in the sky as well,' she insisted.

'The lost village of Penwyn-Mar,' Marc said with wonder and an excited gleam in his eyes.

'Forget the lights in the sky!' Kim said angrily. 'We must go to the police about the whales.'

'No.' Hal was firm. 'We mustn't draw any attention to ourselves. Not now at least.'

'Attention?' Marc had never heard Hal speak like this before.

'If we call in the police, then they'll close down Arthur's Bay while they investigate. Bang go my windsurfing lessons, and Blaise's speedboats, and half of Penwyn-Mar's tourist revenue, too,' he told them truthfully enough. 'It's exactly what Broderick Rune would want.'

'I can't believe that you can be so heartless,' Kim said incredulously. 'Putting your own income above the welfare of the whales.'

'I didn't say that,' Hal said. 'But we'll investigate by ourselves, OK?'

Colette looked warily out at the sea, remembering the whales' sad song of the previous night when she had encountered Hal on the beach and had seen Elenore wracked with pain and distress. 'Maybe we should stay out of the water anyway,' she said fearfully. 'It could be dangerous . . .'

'I can handle the sea,' Hal told her confidently, and led the way back up the beach. As he did so, no one noticed him unzip the front of his wet suit, and slip the microcircuit inside.

He would dispose of it later, he decided, when the others weren't around to see him do so. After all, it was no longer necessary. It had served its purpose. It had found the one he had been looking for . . .

Dateline: Caer Cliffs;
Wednesday 26 August; 16.54.

'You cannot do this!' Elenore said to the infuriatingly supercilious Malvaine, as soon as she, Rebecca and Colette had reached the dig. Malvaine took off his dark glasses, and stared down at her.

'On the contrary, Miss Morgan, we *are* doing this,' he said. His tone was dark and silken, and malicious. Behind him bulldozers were already ploughing up the earth, destroying all the precious work that Elenore and her team had put into the excavation.

'This is an important archaeological site!' Rebecca protested. 'It has to be excavated carefully, slowly.'

'Yeah,' agreed Joey, who, until he had developed his crush on Elenore, hadn't shown even the slightest interest in archaeology. 'What you're doing just don't make sense! Take your time, buster!'

Malvaine looked down his nose at Joey with even more contempt than he had shown for Elenore. It was clear that he wasn't particularly impressed by a slum kid from the Bronx, who was dressed in streetwise clothes and had a bad attitude problem.

'Unfortunately Mr Rune doesn't have that much time,' he said, and Rebecca was curious to note a tiny touch of sadness in Malvaine's voice.

'Look, can't we just talk to him?' Rebecca asked, without much hope of gaining a positive response. 'I'm sure he'd listen to reason.'

'Mr Rune will not grant you or anyone else an audience,' Malvaine stated categorically.

'But–'

'That is final!'

'We might as well give up,' Elenore said sadly as she, Rebecca and Joey started to walk away from the site and Malvaine returned to directing the digging operations. 'You can't fight Broderick Rune.'

'I can't understand why he's doing all this,' Rebecca said. 'I thought it was him who first employed you to investigate the site.'

'Well, sort of,' Elenore said. 'I actually contacted *him* first of all. I was sure that there would be some sort of fortress or encampment at Penwyn-Mar. And as it was on his land I had to ask permission to dig there.'

'And he gave it to you? Just like that?' Joey asked. 'From what I hear of the guy that's not the kind of thing he's likely to do.'

'He didn't at first,' she told them. 'In fact he refused point-blank. But I wrote to him again and told him that there might be a connection with King Arthur. As soon as I mentioned King Arthur he completely changed his tune. He said I could dig wherever I wanted in Penwyn-Mar.'

'But you've never met him?' Rebecca asked.

'No. All the negotiations were done through Malvaine. And I guess we never will meet him now.'

Rebecca shook her head. 'Joey and I don't give up that easy,' she announced. 'We are going to get an audience with the high-and-mighty Broderick Rune. And this is how we're going to do it . . .'

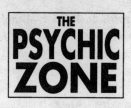

THE PSYCHIC ZONE

5

Sailing to Lyonesse

Dateline: Balan's Bay;
Thursday 27 August; 08.00.

Rebecca threw back her head, enjoying the feel of the sea spray on her face and the wind blowing back her long auburn hair. It had been a long time since she'd been in a speedboat, and it was now that she realised how much she missed those annual family holidays on Lake Michigan with her mom and her late father.

As the speedboat skimmed along the waves, *en route* for Lyonesse, Rebecca glanced back at her two passengers. Joey was looking distinctly ill-at-ease, clutching his stomach and with a peculiar greenish tinge to his face. Speedboat sailing hadn't exactly been a regular event in the life of the Harlem slum kid, and Rebecca guessed correctly that the bobbing up-and-down motion of the boat wasn't doing his stomach any favours – especially as they had sneaked out early when the rest of Tristam Cottage was sleeping and they'd only had the chance to grab a quick bite of toast.

Elenore, on the other hand, seemed tired and distracted, as if she had been awake all night. Colette still hadn't told Rebecca about her nocturnal encounter on the beach, but if she had done, Rebecca would immediately have suspected that that was where Elenore had been last night.

'Say, how did you persuade Blaise to hire you out this speedboat?' Joey asked, as Rebecca sharply altered course and he felt his stomach lurch. 'You're only fifteen.'

'I got Elenore to say that she was piloting it,' she replied, raising her voice to try and make herself heard above the roar of the engine. 'He seemed quite happy with that.'

'I imagine that he couldn't be bothered to ask too many questions this early in the morning,' Elenore said, with a weak smile.

'We had to leave early,' Rebecca said. 'In another half-hour or so the windsurfers will be out and we'll be spotted.'

'What's the difference?' Elenore said. 'We'll be spotted as soon as we reach the island anyway.'

'Not the way I'm going,' Rebecca said and made another adjustment to the steering. The boat slowed down a little as she approached the island.

Lyonesse island had originally been used by the War Department way back in the 1940s, when the Government had established a defence post there in anticipation of a German invasion. After the war it had been deserted for many years, until an enterprising developer in the 70s developed it into a theme park, complete with its own aquarium and marina. It was then that it had got its present name of Lyonesse, the name of that fabled land which, like Atlantis, had sunk beneath the sea. According to Aunt Annie it had been something of a tacky place, but it had brought in valuable tourist revenue, which was why there had been so much bad feeling when Broderick Rune had arrived, bought the place up and made it into his very own, private, off-limits island.

They were almost at the island now, and Rebecca cut the engine down to a *put-put-put* sound as she guided it into a small rocky cove.

Elenore looked about nervously. There was no sign of any guards or security forces, but by all accounts Broderick Rune employed a small private army to ensure that his solitude was never disturbed.

'I don't understand,' she said, as Joey helped her out of the boat and they stepped ashore. 'Why aren't there any guards?'

'There doesn't need to be,' Rebecca said, cheerfully, as she moored the boat. She pointed up the beach. 'Take a look.'

A fence of barbed-wire blocked their way.

Beyond that there was a weather-worn wooden notice, whose legend read:

MINISTRY OF DEFENCE

KEEP OUT

DANGER

'I don't understand,' Elenore said, and then raised a hand to her forehead. She had the beginnings of a severe headache.

'It's a minefield, left over from the Second World War,' Rebecca told her simply. 'That's why Broderick Rune doesn't need any guards on this side of the island.'

'That's terrible,' Elenore said, with feeling, as she watched Joey take a pair of wire-cutters from out of the speedboat. 'I thought there'd been a call for a worldwide ban on those kinds of things.'

'Broderick Rune isn't the sort of guy who follows rules,' Rebecca said. 'And yes, it is terrible – but not for us.'

'But how are we going to get past them?'

Joey grinned and pushed theatrically past the two girls. 'That, Elenore, is where Yours Truly comes in,' he announced. He knelt down and started to attack the barbed-wire with the wire-cutters.

While Joey set about his work, they were all three of them unaware that they were, in fact, being watched. Rebecca had been mistaken when she had assumed that Broderick Rune would have no security on this side of the island. Concealed in a tiny cleft in a rock, a hidden camera was watching their every movement.

Dateline: Arthur's Bay;
Thursday 27 August; 09.19.

'It's no use, Marc, I can't find them anywhere,' Colette said disconsolately as she met up with him on the beach. 'I thought they might be up at the dig, but there's no sign of them – just Rune's men, turning the place into one big hole in the ground.'

'And they're not at Grail Hallows Point either,' Marc said. He was wearing his windsurfing wet suit, but he hadn't been out sailing yet. He was much too concerned about the missing Rebecca and Joey. He looked to the east and towards Balan's Bay. 'You don't think they've gone up there, do you,' he asked.

Colette paused for a moment and then shook her head. 'No,' she said with certainty. 'They know about the quicksands up there. That was the first thing Aunt Annie warned us about when we all came down here.'

'Yeah, I guess not,' Marc agreed. 'Bec can be pretty wilful at times, but she isn't a fool.'

'Marc, I'm worried. I've got a very bad feeling about all this.'

Marc looked strangely at Colette. There was a

time once when even he would have doubted what Colette called her 'hunches', but she had proved him wrong time and time again in the past.

'Colette, you've always been able to sense where Joey is before,' he reminded her. 'How about trying it now?'

'Don't you think I haven't been doing that for the past half-hour or so?' she asked with a tremor in her voice. 'But there's nothing, and that's what makes it so bad!'

'Try once more – just for me,' he said, and then added: 'I'm as worried about them as you are, you know.'

Colette smiled weakly and, for some reason she couldn't quite explain, she turned away from Marc and looked seawards, towards Pendragon Rock and then past that to the horizon. Her eyes misted over as she tried to empty her head of all thoughts but one: *Joey. Joey. Joey.*

Nothing. Just the noise of the waves as they rushed to shore.

'Once more, Colette,' Marc urged.

Joey. Joey. Joey . . .

Colette was about to turn helplessly back to Marc, tears in her eyes, when something jolted her. Marc rushed up to her.

'What is it, Colette?' he demanded. 'What is it that you can sense out there? Is it Joey?'

'Joey? No, it's not Joey,' Colette said, and her lips were quivering with fear. 'It's evil, Marc! Great evil, evil, *evil . . .'*

'Hey, what are you two up to?'

Colette was jolted out of her semi-trance and looked to see Hal swimming through the waters towards them. Neither Marc nor she had seen him out there before, but then they had been so preoccupied with their own concerns that that was hardly surprising.

'Where have you come from?' Marc asked.

Hal stood up in the water and waded through the shallows towards them. He didn't come out of the water completely however, and the waves gently lapped at his ankles.

'Out for a morning swim,' he told them. 'By Pendragon Rock.'

Marc shaded his eyes from the morning and looked to the lighthouse. It was a good mile's swim away at least. Surely even a powerful swimmer like Hal couldn't have managed that distance and not show even the slightest sign of exhaustion? Was Hal really telling them the truth?

Hal asked them again what they were doing, and when Marc was going to come out for his windsurfing lesson. He seemed unconcerned about Rebecca and Joey's disappearance.

'They'll be all right,' he assured them. 'Like you say, Rebecca's a sensible girl, and I'm sure that Joey can look after himself. Heck, if you can stay alive on the streets of Harlem then you can survive anything!'

'But I've always had a vague idea where Joey is before,' Colette told him, anxiously.

'Maybe they've gone to see Elenore Morgan?' Hal suggested.

'That's just the trouble,' Colette said. 'I called at the hostel where she's been staying and she's gone as well.'

'Elenore? Gone?' Hal's concern was genuine now. 'I – we must find her.'

Marc was taken aback by Hal's sudden change of mood. 'What's the big deal, Hal?' he asked. 'You yourself have just said that Bec and Joey are probably OK. What's so special about Elenore?'

Hal gave Marc a look which he'd never seen before. It wasn't quite a superior look, or a condescending glance, but somehow an inability to understand how Marc could be just so stupid. Then that look passed, and Hal was the same old Hal again.

'You don't understand,' he said finally. 'Elenore is – different, that's all . . .'

'Different?' asked Colette. 'How is she different?'

Hal chose not to answer. 'Where is Kim?' he wanted to know.

'I'm meeting her later at The Excalibur Express,' Marc said, referring to Blaise's tacky café on the beach. 'We're going to examine Starshine.'

There was a look of horror on Hal's face at the news. 'You're going to do *what*?'

'Kim managed to bribe Blaise into putting Starshine into his chest-freezer to preserve her,' Marc said. 'She's a zoologist and I'm a biology student. Maybe we can find out what happened to her.'

'Let's just hope the Health and Safety Department don't get to hear about that,' Colette said, in spite of the serious look on Hal's face.

'She can't do that,' Hal said, even though Marc reminded him that it had been his suggestion that they, rather than the police, look into the mystery of the whales. And then Marc realised that Hal had only said that so that there would be no official inquiry.

'I must go and see her,' Hal determined.

'I saw her at the hostel when I went looking for Elenore,' Colette told him. 'She's probably still there.'

'Then that's where I'll go,' Hal said, and turned to dive back into the sea.

'You're *swimming* there?' Marc asked in amazement. 'The hostel's only a ten-minute walk along the beach.'

'I'll swim,' Hal said and, without further ado, splashed back into the water and swam away with long powerful strokes.

Marc breathed a sigh of surprise and turned back to Colette, who was watching Hal's departing figure moving like a fish in the waters.

'Now, what do you make of that?' he asked her, and then saw the serious look on Colette's face. 'What's wrong, Colette?'

'I sensed evil, great evil,' she remembered. 'And then Hal appeared.'

'What are you saying?'

'Have you ever seen Hal's feet?'

'Hal's *feet*? Colette, what are you talking about?'

'Did you notice the way Hal kept himself in the shallows when he was talking to us just then?' she asked Marc. 'The water covered his ankles.'

'Yes,' Marc said, uncertain where Colette was leading.

'And the other night when I saw him down on the beach, just before I heard those explosions,' Colette remembered. 'I laughed when I saw him try and put on his jeans over his trainers.'

'That is a bit daft, yes,' Marc agreed.

'Have you ever seen him barefooted?' Colette asked, and Marc admitted that he hadn't. Even when out windsurfing Hal would always wear trainers or windsurfing boots. Colette nodded wisely, took off her own shoes and socks, and paddled into the water to the spot where Hal had been standing. She pointed down in the sand.

'It's impossible,' Marc breathed.

'No, it's true,' Colette said. 'What is it Rebecca's always saying? Always trust the evidence of your own eyes. And the evidence is staring us right in the face!'

There in the spot where Hal had been standing were his footprints. But they were not normal footprints, like the ones Marc now made as he took off his own sandals and joined Colette in the shallows.

They were staring down at the footprints of some marine animal, webbed and large. They were staring down not at the footprints left by a human being.

They were staring down at the footprints of an alien!

THE PSYCHIC ZONE

6

The Prisoners of Lyonesse

Dateline: Lyonesse;
Thursday 27 August; 09.33.

Just as Marc and Colette were making their terrible discovery on the beach and wondering what manner of creature Hal really was, Joey had finally managed to cut a hole wide enough for them in the barbed-wire fencing which led to the minefield. He stood back, surveying his work with pride.

'Back home in Harlem, I was always the best in the gang for breaking and entering,' he bragged. 'Nice to know that even with months of posh schooling in England, the old talents never leave you!'

'I don't think Elenore really wants to know that much about your sordid past, Joey,' Rebecca said with a grin.

Elenore winked at Joey. 'You can tell me more about it later,' she said, and Joey blushed once again. She turned back and looked at the minefield ahead of them. The ground had been raked and levelled, and there was no way of telling where the landmines had been laid. Beyond the minefield, past a small wood, they could see the building that had once been the marina and now formed part of the official residence of Broderick Rune.

'How do we get through that?' Elenore asked. 'One false step and we're dead meat.'

'Trust Joey,' Rebecca said. 'OK, Joey – go for it!'

'It'll be a piece of cake,' Joey said confidently, and then his tone became suddenly serious. 'Now both of you girls do exactly what I do, OK? Put your feet *exactly* where I put mine. Otherwise, they'll be scraping you off the floor from now until doomsday.'

'We trust you, Joey,' Elenore said, as Joey turned back and looked closely at the minefield. He took a deep breath and moved – one step at a time – concentrating for long seconds before putting his foot down on the ground. Dowsing for Roman pottery – even for microcircuits – had been one matter, and something he even regarded as a minor party trick. But he knew that this was a matter of life or death. If he screwed up now, if he failed to locate the presence of just one hidden landmine, then all three of them would be blown to kingdom come.

'Are you sure you know what you're doing, Joey?'

Elenore asked as she followed in his footsteps.

'Sure I'm sure,' Joey said – unsurely – and stopped for a moment.

Joey . . . Joey . . .

Rebecca noticed his hesitation and asked him what was the matter. Joey shook his head.

'Nothing,' he said. 'I thought I heard someone calling out my name. It was probably my imagination.'

'It was the wind, nothing more,' said Elenore.

'You must concentrate,' Rebecca urged him. 'Let yourself be distracted by anything and we're all done for.'

Just under a mile away, Colette's eyes misted over as she tried to empty her head of all thoughts but one: *Joey. Joey. Joey . . .* Nothing. Just the noise of the waves as they rushed to shore . . .

'OK, OK, don't hassle me, right?'

Joey . . . Joey . . .

Joey willed the voice out of his brain and carried on negotiating the minefield.

The atmosphere was tense, with a heavy silence between Rebecca and Elenore, until Elenore spoke, 'Look at it this way,' she said glumly. 'We can't go back now.'

Joey finally reached the end of the minefield, turned with a triumphant look to the girls, and offered out his hand to Elenore. She jumped over the last half-metre of ground towards him.

'See, I told you I could do it!' he bragged and swelled his chest with pride.

'Joey, I never doubted you,' said an enormously relieved Elenore.

'Oh yeah?' Joey might have had a schoolboy crush on Elenore but even he wasn't that easily fooled. The sweat on her brow gave her away. She had been petrified walking through the minefield.

'Now what?' Rebecca asked, as she looked up at the big mansion in the centre of the island. Getting here had been the easy part, she reflected. Now they had to gain access to Broderick Rune's domain itself.

Joey sighed in mock despair, and shoved his hands into the pockets of his jeans. 'Jeez!' he complained. 'Does a guy have to do everything himself around here?'

*Dateline: Broderick Rune's Command
Chamber, Lyonesse;
Thursday 27 August; 10.00.*

From the comfort of his marble desk Broderick Rune watched the bank of video screens on the far wall of his study. Each screen displayed a picture of a different area of Lyonesse: from the harbour where he would sometimes embark on his private yacht, to the tiniest room in his vast palace of a house.

He operated a touch-sensitive control set into the marble of the desk, and all the screens dimmed except for one: the one showing Joey, Rebecca and Elenore leaving the minefield.

A faint smile played around his lips as he looked up at his two companions who were standing on either side of the desk.

'It seems that Malvaine was right, after all,' Broderick Rune said. 'Bring the boy to me.'

'And the others?' asked Malvaine, who was standing at his master's right hand.

'The two girls? Kill them.'

'At once,' Malvaine said, and grinned. 'It will be a pleasure, sir.'

'On second thoughts, bring them to me alive,' Broderick Rune said. 'They may prove useful bargaining tools should the boy prove to be uncooperative.'

'As you wish, sir,' replied Malvaine, although it was clear from the tone of his voice that he was very disappointed indeed.

Dateline: Penwyn-Mar youth hostel;
Thursday 27 August; 10.01.

Marc and Colette burst through the doors of the youth hostel where Kim was staying and, ignoring the protests of the *concierge* who said that they couldn't enter the building without a security pass, they rushed across the entrance hall and took the stairs two at a time.

'Which one is her room?' Marc asked.

'Twenty-three,' Colette said, and led the way. 'But why do we have to see her so urgently? You're due to meet her later at the café.'

'Because later might be much too late,' Marc said, 'if Hal gets here before us.'

'But we still don't *know* what Hal is, or what he's doing at Penwyn-Mar,' said Colette, who was intent on seeing the best in people – even now.

'Up to no good, that's what,' Marc said as he pounded on the door of Room Twenty-three. 'He's probably responsible for the deaths of those whales. Maybe even the explosions you say you heard.'

'And Elenore too?' Colette asked. She wondered why Marc looked puzzled, until she realised that she still hadn't told him about seeing Elenore on the beach.

The door opened and Kim was standing there, a bemused look on her face. 'Where's the fire? she asked, looking down at Marc's wet suit, which seemed totally out-of-place in the clean and tidy surroundings of the youth hostel.

'Hal – have you seen him today?' he asked, panting for breath: it had been a long run from the beach to the hostel, especially since they had wanted to outrace Hal.

'Of course not,' she replied, not quite sure whether Marc was implying something or not. 'Why, should I have done?'

'You don't understand,' Colette said, 'Hal isn't quite like you or me. He's – different . . .'

'Different? What on earth are you two on about?'

Just then one of the girls who was rooming on Kim's floor walked by. Marc and Colette recognised her as one of Elenore's co-workers on the dig. She'd heard the tail-end of their conversation and now butted in with her own comment.

'Too right he's different,' she said. 'Who in his right mind would want to go and eat at a greasy spoon like Blaise's this early in the morning?'

'A greasy spoon?' For a second Marc and Colette wasn't sure what she was talking about . . . and then the penny dropped.

'He's fooled us all!' Marc realised. 'We thought he was coming for Kim. But he's gone to The Excalibur Express!'

'That's OK,' Colette said. 'He won't be able to get in. The café doesn't open until well past noon.'

'Oh yes he will,' Marc realised. 'He works for Blaise. Blaise will have given him a set of keys.'

'Would either of you two care to tell me what is going on around here?' Kim said, irritably.

Colette's face fell. 'Trust me, Kim, you are not going to like this one little bit!'

Dateline: Lyonesse;
Thursday 27 August; 11.15.

Joey smiled smugly as he twirled the twisted piece of wire in the lock of the double gates, and they sprang open with a satisfying *click*! He turned back to the girls.

'Shall I show you round?' he asked grandly, like a butler offering a tour of his master's stately home; but Rebecca and Kim had already walked past him and into the complex behind the gates.

'This must be all that's left of the old marina,' Rebecca realised as she saw the rows of seats set around three sides of a large tank, which looked about the size of a tennis court. The fourth wall of the tank was formed by a gate, leading out into the open sea. 'It must be where people came to see the orcas and the seals put through their paces.'

'Yuk, fancy living your life jumping through hoops for humans,' Joey said with distaste. 'What kind of life is that for a whale that's known the freedom of the ocean?'

'Freedom . . .' Elenore repeated the word strangely. 'Freedom is a wonderful thing . . .'

Joey frowned. 'Are you OK, Elenore?' he asked, and reached and felt her hand. It was cold and clammy to the touch.

'I'm . . . I'm fine,' Elenore said, although Joey wasn't quite certain whether she was telling the truth or not. 'It's just that you mentioning freedom. It reminded me of something.'

'Reminded you of what?'

'I'm not sure . . .' Elenore admitted and told Joey not to worry.

'I don't understand why he hasn't bulldozed this place like he did the rest of the theme park, and built on it,' Rebecca said, looking over the walls of the erstwhile marine park to the mansion in the centre of the island, which was Broderick Rune's home.

'That's maybe because it's still in use,' said Joey excitedly and pointed to the waters inside the tank. Several orcas were swimming about there and they looked up with anticipation as Joey peered over the edge at them. They squawked and honked at him.

'Hey, you think I'd be able to talk to them?' Joey asked. Rebecca nodded and joined him and Elenore by the tank.

'If anyone could, then you could,' she said. 'But why is Rune keeping them here? It doesn't make sense. Just as his cancelling the dig doesn't make sense.'

'Do you think he has something to do with the whales that Kim discovered?' Elenore asked, and then yelped as she felt something sharp dig into the hollow of her back – the barrel of a rifle.

'Perhaps you would like to ask Mr Rune yourself,' Malvaine said, and instructed the three jack-booted and armed guards to take them away for their audience with Broderick Rune.

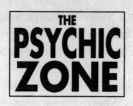

7

An Audience with Broderick Rune

*Dateline: Broderick Rune's Command
Chamber, Lyonesse;
Thursday 27 August; 14.11.*

Rebecca, Joey and Elenore were escorted roughly, at gunpoint, out of the marine park and up the steps which led to Broderick Rune's mansion.

The mansion – also called Lyonesse – dominated the island. A mock-Gothic monstrosity (even though it had only been built a few years ago) it was, as Joey so adequately described it on the long march up there, 'pure Addams family'.

But when they entered through the great oaken doors into the grand hall, they were surprised at the ultra-modernity of the building's interior. Computer-generated paintings hung on the walls – paintings which, Rebecca knew, could be changed at the flick of a switch. Where another hallway might be furnished with statues or period chairs and tables, the hallway of Lyonesse was decorated with holograms of some of the most famous statues in history: Michelangelo's *David*, the *Venus de Milo*, Rodin's *Thinker*. Whatever else Broderick Rune was, Rebecca reflected as they were taken by Malvaine and the guards, he was a man of enormous wealth and immense good taste.

They reached a final set of double doors and Malvaine pressed his hand against a light sensor. There was a brief buzz of machinery as the computer system identified his palm print, and then the doors sighed open, allowing them access to the great man himself.

Rebecca, Joey and Elenore had no idea what to expect as they entered the massive marble room, bare except for Rune's control desk and a bank of video monitors which covered one entire wall of the chamber. Neither Joey nor Rebecca had ever seen a newspaper photograph of the computer wizard, and even Elenore had only ever communicated with him through Malvaine. Despite themselves, they were visibly shocked by what they saw.

Broderick Rune was a frail-looking old man – of at least seventy years, Rebecca guessed, although she wouldn't have been surprised if he'd been a lot older. He was seated in a futuristic-looking wheelchair, obviously the highest state-of-the-art machine that money could buy.

For a moment Rebecca and Joey found themselves each thinking of General Axford, the principal at their school. He, too, was confined to a wheelchair, but whereas his disability had seemed to have given him an inner vigour and strength, Rune appeared a shadow of the man he must have once been. For all her feelings towards the man, Rebecca at that moment felt immensely sorry for him.

And it wasn't just the wheelchair that made her heart go out to him. Broderick Rune was dressed as impeccably as Malvaine, but the rouge on his hollow cheeks, and the black hair which was so obviously dyed, made him look almost laughable – if the spectacle of an obviously ill and old man wasn't so sad.

'Welcome, Miss Morgan. We meet at last,' he said. His voice was cracked and ancient, and Joey realised with horror that he was talking through a microphone hidden somewhere deep inside his throat. It occurred to Joey that Rune's entire body could be riddled with cancer.

Broderick Rune turned next to him and Rebecca. 'And good day to you, Miss Storm, Mr Williams.'

'How do you know our names?' Joey demanded.

'Mr Rune makes it his business to know everything.'

For the first time they realised that there was someone else in the room in addition to themselves, their guards, and Broderick Rune and Malvaine.

The newcomer walked up to them, a woman who looked totally out-of-place in the hi-tech surroundings of Lyonesse. She was in her mid-forties, with long and frizzy greying hair, dressed in a colourful kaftan with strings of ethnic jewellery around her neck, and each of her fingers was weighed down by a gaudy piece of costume jewellery. She moved out of the corner as lithely as a cat, and she smelt strongly of incense and patchouli oil.

'Who says that there aren't any hippies any more?' Joey half-whispered to Rebecca.

'She looks familiar,' Elenore muttered, and racked her memory to try and recall where she had seen the woman before. 'Don't I know you from somewhere?' she asked.

'You may know me as Madame Morgana,' the woman announced grandly.

Elenore nodded her head and smiled, before turning back to Rebecca and Joey. 'Now I remember,' she told them. 'I met her at Cambridge once. She was supposedly an expert on Arthurian legends, until she was dismissed as a fraud when she faked an old document purporting to point to the location of Arthur's grave. She's as nutty as a fruitcake! Her name isn't even Morgana – she just went and stole the name of Arthur's half-sister.'

Morgana glared at Elenore through eyes heavy with mascara, and looked first to Malvaine for support (he was smirking) and then to Broderick Rune. Rune activated a control on his wheelchair and approached Elenore, Rebecca and Joey.

'Madame Morgana is a woman of great knowledge, and you shall learn respect for her,' he told them, and even though his voice was weak there was real menace in it too.

'She's a charlatan and a fake,' Elenore insisted. 'She'll say anything and come up with any new crackpot theory if the money's right. How much have you paid her, Broderick Rune?'

'That is not for you to know,' Rune said. 'Now. You have trespassed on my land. I want to know why.'

'You've closed down the dig, the very dig that you wanted to go ahead,' Elenore said. 'I want to know why.'

'The dig has served its purpose, as have you, Miss Morgan,' Rune said. 'I found the clue I was looking for – or rather you and your companions did.'

For a moment the three of them had no idea what Rune was talking about . . . and then the penny dropped for Rebecca.

'The microcircuit! That was what you were looking for,' she said. Broderick Rune nodded his head.

'Then why didn't you try and take it from us when we discovered it?' Joey asked and tried to remember when he'd last seen the chip. He recalled Colette passing it to Hal. What had he done with it?

'The microcircuit wasn't what I wanted,' Broderick Rune corrected him. 'It was merely a clue, a confirmation that my theories were correct, after all.'

'Your theories?' Rebecca asked. There was a curious gleam in Rune's watery eyes, the gleam of a man consumed by hope.

'That there is something else at Penwyn-Mar, something truly, truly wonderful,' he said. 'Perhaps something alien to our own Twentieth Century, Miss Storm. And far superior.'

'*Alien?*' Rebecca thought about the lights that they had seen in the sky on their first day in Cornwall. She remembered the legends of the lost village of Penwyn-Mar.

'The people of Penwyn-Mar live to a great age, Miss Storm, never beset by illness or disease,' Broderick Rune continued. 'Have you ever wondered why?'

'There could be a thousand-and-one reasons,' Rebecca insisted, recalling her conversation a few days ago with Colette. 'A good diet, something in the water . . .'

'And Madame Morgana here has pointed out to me Penwyn-Mar's numerous connections with King Arthur.'

'Arthur's Bay, Grail Hallows' Point,' Morgana reeled off a list of names. 'Pendragon Rock, Balan's Bay . . .'

'Not forgetting Ye Olde Round Table Tea Shoppe,' Rebecca countered sarcastically. 'And The Excalibur Express, The Lady in the Lake Laundromat . . .'

'There are places as far apart as Scotland and

Wales, Cornwall and Cumbria, all of which claim some sort of link with Arthur,' Elenore told them. 'If they're all true then King Arthur is buried in at least half-a-dozen places all over the country.'

'Yeah,' said Joey who had no idea whether Elenore was right but was determined not to be left out of the conversation. 'So what makes Penwyn-Mar so special?'

'Madame Morgana here has convinced me that a great treasure lies buried beneath Penwyn-Mar,' Broderick Rune told them.

'The lost village?' Joey asked with wonder in his eyes.

'Arthur never existed,' Rebecca insisted to Rune. 'At least not the Arthur you're thinking of. He was just a war chief – nothing more and nothing less.'

'Arthur isn't the treasure that lies beneath Penwyn-Mar, you foolish slip of a girl,' Broderick Rune snapped.

'Don't you go calling me "a slip of a girl",' Rebecca snapped back herself. Broderick Rune chose to ignore her.

'What I seek is something much more precious than that. I seek nothing less than the Holy Grail itself!'

'The what?' Joey piped up, somewhat destroying the portentous atmosphere that had fallen on the room.

'One of the holiest treasures of the Isles of Britain,' replied Madame Morgana.

'Gee, thanks! That tells me a lot!'

'It's supposedly the cup which Jesus Christ drank from at the Last Supper,' Elenore told Joey. 'Another myth. Such a thing couldn't exist.'

'Ah, but the Grail cup is much older than that,' Morgana said. 'And it contains no less than the secret of eternal life.'

Now everything fell into place for Rebecca, and she couldn't help but feel sympathy for the poor, wheelchair-bound figure of Broderick Rune. 'I understand now,' she said. 'You're an ill man, Mr Rune, and I'm very sorry about that. But this crazy woman's taking you for a ride. And you'll never find the secret of eternal life, because there isn't one.'

But Broderick Rune wasn't listening. His eyes were glazed over with the madness of a dying man clutching at straws. 'Imagine a cure to all the ills of the world,' he said. 'A planet rid of disease.'

'You could have spent your life trying to cure those ills,' Joey pointed out, 'instead of designing software programs for the army.'

'The man who held such a secret would be master of the world,' Rune continued. 'And I, Broderick Rune, shall be that man. I, Broderick Rune, shall seize the Grail cup and drink deep of its waters of eternal life.'

Rebecca turned to Joey and Elenore. 'Can you believe this guy?' she asked. 'I didn't think even B-movie actors spoke that way any more!'

The remark was meant to disguise her own fear. Broderick Rune was mad, Rebecca knew, and that meant that he was very dangerous indeed. She glanced over to the closed double doors. Three guards were stationed there. She could never hope to make a run for it with them and Malvaine there.

But Broderick Rune hadn't finished yet. He pointed a long and bony finger at Joey. 'And this is the child who shall help me find the Holy Grail,' he announced. 'This is the child who shall bring to me the secret of eternal life!'

Dateline: The Excalibur Express Penwyn-Mar;
Thursday 27 August; 12.30.

Marc had been steeling himself for breaking down the door of The Excalibur Express, but when he, Colette and Kim reached the café, they discovered that the door was already open. Blaise was standing there, a look of blank incomprehension on his face.

'What happened?' Marc asked, and pushed past the man into the café itself. He headed straight for the kitchen.

Just as he had suspected, the lid of the large chest-freezer had been left open. He looked inside. Frozen packs of food were already thawing out and there was an unpleasant stench in the air. Of the killer whale, there was no sign.

'He's taken her,' Kim said, half in tears.

'Of course he has,' Colette said. 'The whale was

evidence that he's been killing them.'

'We've no proof of that,' Marc pointed out, although in his heart of hearts he believed Colette.

'Then why take her away?' Kim asked sensibly. 'For some reason Hal doesn't want us to know why the whales are growing younger and younger and then dying.'

'We have to find him,' Marc determined. 'Blaise, would you know where Hal would go?'

Blaise shrugged his shoulders. He was only the boatkeeper and local enterpreneur, he said – and a very successful one at that, he added. How should he be expected to know about the comings and goings of the people he employed on a casual basis for the summer?

Marc asked the same question of Kim. She proved to be almost as unhelpful.

'I've told you before, I've not known him for long,' she reminded him. 'Whenever I did arrange to meet him, it was always at the boathouse, where Blaise keeps his speedboats and his windsurfing rigs.

It was a long shot, but, as that was all they had to go on, Marc decided they should take it. They raced down the beach the one mile to Arthur's Bay.

'There he is!' Colette shouted as they turned the corner. Just out of reach, Hal was dragging a powerboat down to the sea's edge. He saw them and there was a wild look in his seagreen eyes.

'Keep away!' he called out. 'You don't under-stand!'

'Maybe not!' Marc cried back. 'But you're blasted well going to make us understand!'

He started to run across the beach towards Hal, but the windsurfer was far too quick for him. Hal leapt into the powerboat, pulled on the throttle, and he was off in a plume of spray and foam leaving Marc standing alone on the shore.

Marc turned to Blaise who had just managed to catch up with him. 'Blaise, have you got another boat?' he demanded. 'We have to go after him.'

Blaise shook his head. 'I've only three, and Hal's run off with one of them,' he told him. 'And the other one I hired out to some tourists who wanted to take a day trip to Saint Michael's Mount.'

'Well, what about the third boat, Blaise?' Colette pressed him. 'Where's that?'

Blaise turned his face away from Marc and Colette.

'I hired that out to Miss Storm and her two friends this morning,' he told them sheepishly. 'They wanted to go to Lyonesse. I–'

'What!' In all the excitement Marc had forgotten that he and Colette had originally set out this morning to look for Rebecca and Joey. 'You let them go by themselves to see Broderick Rune?'

'I told 'em not to . . .'

'Yeah, but I bet you still took their money all the same,' Marc said bitterly. He looked out to sea. 'Where do you think he's heading?'

'It's obvious, isn't it?' Kim said. 'Pendragon Rock.'

'The place where we first saw those lights, and heard the explosions,' Colette realised.

'He'll smash my boat to pieces on those rocks,' Blaise said, wondering whether he'd paid his insurance premiums lately.

'Not him,' Marc said. 'He knows the sea too well.'

'So what do we do now?' asked Colette. 'Can we call in the coastguard?'

'And tell them what? That an alien, looking like a man but with webbed feet, has just run off with the frozen carcass of a baby killer whale that isn't really a baby at all? Get real, Colette! All we can do now is wait!'

THE PSYCHIC ZONE

8

Escape Into Danger

Dateline: Lyonesse;
Thursday 27 August; 14.27.

'I can't do it,' said Joey. He sat with Rebecca and Elenore in the large cell into which Broderick Rune had locked them to consider what their response would be to his demands.

'No,' Elenore said firmly. 'It's not that you can't do it. It's that you *won't* do it.'

Joey looked curiously at Elenore. They'd been locked in this cell for about an hour now and, as cells went, he supposed that it wasn't too bad. Not that he'd had much experience, of course, apart from that one time when the NYPD had picked him up off the street for spray-graffittiing a subway train and they'd banged him up for five too-long minutes as a salutary lesson never to do it again.

Even Rebecca was staying calm. But Elenore? No way. The minute that door had slammed shut, she started panicking and suffering violent mood changes: one minute up and optimistic, the next down and miserable. It was almost as if, as soon as that door had clanged shut, another door had opened up in her mind, bringing to the fore memories she'd rather not be reminded of.

'Hang on a minute,' he said. 'You're asking me to help out this guy who's just gone and locked all three of us up? Why should I do that?'

'He'd let us all go then,' Elenore said simply, and looked around the cell. 'I hate this place. It reminds me of – somewhere . . .'

'Where?' asked Rebecca curiously.

'That's just it,' Elenore began sobbing. 'I don't know.'

'We don't even know if this Grail thing exists,' Joey pointed out practically. 'And if it does, I certainly wouldn't want the likes of Broderick Rune to have it.'

'But Joey, think what good it could do for the world,' Elenore said, pleading with him now to reconsider his objection to Rune's plan. 'Eternal life! Or at the very least a cure for disease. No more cancer, no more AIDS, no more suffering! Would you deny the world that?'

'And you seriously think Rune would use it in the way you think?' Joey asked. 'No way. He'd use it to hold the world to ransom. He said as much.'

'Joey's right, Elenore,' Rebecca said sadly.

'People like Broderick Rune just can't be trusted.'

'But we have to get out!' Elenore was becoming hysterical now. She stood up and started pacing around the cell. 'I can't stand it in here any longer!'

Elenore started to shake uncontrollably. 'Calm down!' Rebecca said, and stood up to hold her in her arms. 'It'll be OK.'

'No, it won't,' Elenore insisted. 'You don't know what it's like to be locked up again!'

'*Again?* Elenore, what do you mean, again?'

Elenore looked up at Rebecca, tears in her eyes. 'That's the whole problem – I don't know what I mean,' she admitted finally. 'There are huge bits of my past which are a complete blank.'

'You mean, like amnesia?' asked Joey, and Elenore nodded. Joey remembered the conversation they had shared at the dig.

'I'm just really impressed that you can remember all those dates and stuff.'

'I wish there were other things I could remember as well.'

'What do you mean?'

'Never mind.'

'I can help you, you know,' he said softly, realising the pain Elenore must be going through.

'Help me? How?'

'I can look into your mind,' he told her, suddenly sounding much older than his thirteen years. 'See things that you've forgotten. Help you to come to terms with what you've lost.'

Elenore looked over to Rebecca for confirmation.

Rebecca nodded. Yes, she said, Joey could do all he said he could – and more besides.

Joey instructed Elenore to sit down on one of the chairs in the cell, and he knelt down before her. He told her to close her eyes, then he closed his own and reached out and touched her forehead.

'Just relax,' Joey said soothingly, as he tried to enter Elenore's subconscious with his conscious mind. 'Don't try and resist. Just relax . . . relax . . .'

Slowly, Joey felt his mind filtering into Elenore's, the synapses and dendrites of his brain connecting with the synapses and dendrites of hers. His mind was in Elenore's now. Elenore's mind was in his. Images of Elenore's past started to flicker across Joey's closed eyes. Voices from her past started to sound in his own ears.

Cambridge. A popular student, if a bit of a loner. A fascination for the Fifth Century, the time of Arturius, the dux bellorum. Working long and hard through the night, because she couldn't sleep. A voice in her head calling out her name . . .

The first time she'd heard of Penwyn-Mar. Somehow knowing that there was an important fort there, even though she'd never set foot there in her life. The voice in her head stronger now, drawing her to the tiny Cornish resort.

A few days ago now. Standing on the beach, looking towards Pendragon Rock and its lighthouse that had been deserted there for years now. Fascinated by it.

No, Joey decided, this wasn't what he wanted. This was all too new, too recent. He pushed further back, seeking out the secrets of Elenore's past that she had hidden so completely even from herself.

Her first day at Cambridge, anxious and afraid, but still surprising her fellow students and her lecturers with her knowledge. And yet there were was one piece of knowledge that always escaped her. What was she doing here? Who was she?

No, willed Joey, further back.

Darkness. The cold clammy embrace of the sea. The sound of waves lapping the shores of an alien sea. Feelings of guilt, of fear, or retribution. Of justice?

A golden chalice, encrusted with rubies and emeralds, and sapphires the colour of the ocean.

The Holy Grail. Eternal life . . .

'It's OK,' said Joey, 'you can open your eyes now.' His voice sounded tired and strained.

'What did you see?' asked Elenore, with growing apprehension. 'What did you learn?'

'Nothing,' Joey lied. 'I saw nothing at all.'

'And we're still trapped in this terrible place,' she moaned, and hugged herself for comfort.

'No, we're not,' said Joey firmly and started to bang on the door of the cell.

'You're going to help Broderick Rune after all?' Elenore asked.

'You're really prepared to help him locate the Grail – or whatever it is he thinks is the Grail?' Rebecca couldn't quite believe that someone like Joey would help a man like Rune.'

'Yes, I am – but on my own terms,' he said, and

shouted out to Malvaine, who was waiting outside, to open up.

'But where is it, Joey?' asked Elenore. 'Where is the Grail?'

'It's been staring at us in the face from the first day any of us came here,' he told them. 'It's under the lighthouse on Pendragon Rock!'

Dateline: Broderick Rune's Control Chamber, Lyonesse; Thursday 27 August; 14.54.

Broderick Rune looked up from his desk as Malvaine ushered Joey into his presence. Madame Morgana was there too, carrying a book of the legends of King Arthur and the Holy Grail. It was the same book through which Kim had been browsing on the beach and Joey wondered whether that was the extent of the charlatan's knowledge. Did she really know what lay beneath the Pendragon lighthouse, or was it merely a fluke that she had brought Broderick Rune to Penwyn-Mar with her promises of eternal life? Joey, like Rebecca, suspected the latter. But it wasn't Morgana that he had to bother about now, but Broderick Rune.

'Well, has the child decided?' he asked Malvaine, but it was Joey who replied.

'I can speak for myself, y'know,' he said peevishly.

Broderick moved closer to Joey and touched him

on the cheek. The old man's touch was gnarled and crabby, and Joey flinched – not just at the feel of his skin against his own, but at the smell of Broderick Rune's breath, foul-smelling and rancid.

'Such fire!' Broderick Rune said appreciatively. 'Such vitality! Such *youth*!' Joey fixed the billionaire with a defiant stare. 'Look, are you going to carry on pawing me all day, or do you want to hear what I've got to say?'

For a moment, Broderick Rune's eyes flashed angrily, and Joey wondered whether he'd gone too far. People had been killed for far less, he imagined. But Joey was in control now, holding what was effectively the power of life or death over Broderick Rune, and Broderick Rune knew it.

'You've reached a decision?' There was hope in Broderick Rune's voice now.

'Sure I have,' Joey said.

'Well, what is it?'

Joey paused for a moment, not so much for dramatic effect, as to make Broderick Rune realise what it was like to want something so desperately and to know that all his billions couldn't buy it for him. It would teach the man a lesson, he reflected.

'Well?' Rune was growing impatient now. 'Tell me what it is that you've decided!'

Behind him, Joey felt Malvaine lay a hand on his shoulder and squeeze it hard. Unlike his master, Malvaine had no hesitation about hurting him.

'OK, I'll do it,' Joey said finally. 'I'll help you to locate the Holy Grail in Penwyn-Mar!'

The joy on Broderick Rune's face was almost too painful to behold, as he clapped his hands together in ecstasy. *At last he would be free from the tyranny of dying!* he told himself. *At last he would prove to the world that he was better than the rest of its miserable population, that he, Broderick Rune, was superhuman.* Even though Joey was not reading his mind, he was certain that those were the very thoughts that Rune was now thinking.

'On two conditions,' Joey said.

Rune eyed him suspiciously.

'First of all, that you release the whales that you're keeping in that pen out there,' he said.

'Of course,' Broderick Rune said. 'With you to help me I no longer need them.'

Joey frowned. 'Need them?'

'Of course,' Malvaine said behind him. 'They were trained to conduct underwater excavations for us. Placing bombs in the places inaccessible to human divers, in Mr Rune's efforts to find the Grail'

You cheap streak of bilgewater! Joey thought, as he realised how many whales must have died in such an operation. They must have been the source of the explosions in the bay that Colette had heard.

'It's a practice I believe the US navy has used as well in the past,' Rune said, without any trace of guilt or remorse. 'Now what is your other condition?'

'That you let my two friends go.'

Broderick Rune chuckled. 'You know I can't do that,' he said. 'With them no longer my prisoners, what guarantee do I have that you'll help me?'

Joey's face fell, and he hoped that he was giving a decent enough impression of looking disappointed. 'Then let at least one of them go,' he asked.

Broderick Rune considered the matter for a moment. 'Very well,' he agreed. 'Which one is it to be?'

'Rebecca,' Joey said. 'Let her return to the mainland.'

Rune nodded his agreement. 'The Morgan woman will stay here,' he said.

'No,' Joey said slyly. 'Let her come with us. She might not have my psychic powers, but she is an archaeologist. She could come in handy.'

Broderick Rune nodded his agreement once again, and Joey breathed a silent sigh of relief. If what he had learnt from Elenore's hidden memories was true then it was vital that she accompany them to Pendragon Rock.

'Then let us begin,' Rune said.

'Release the whales and Rebecca first,' Joey said, 'and then I can get down to trying to find the location of the Grail.'

'You have no idea where it is?'

'Not yet,' Joey lied. It was vital that he stalled Rune long enough for Rebecca to get back to the mainland and raise the alarm with Marc, Colette, Hal and Kim.

'Very well,' Rune said, and wheeled himself over to Malvaine, who had now released Joey from his grip and was standing with Madame Morgana by Rune's desk. 'Release the girl,' Rune commanded

Malvaine, and then added in a whisper which Joey couldn't hear. 'And make sure that she doesn't reach land alive.'

Dateline: Arthur's Bay; Thursday 27 August; 16.16.

Marc had never felt more useless in his life, as he stood in the shallows of Arthur's Bay looking out to the Pendragon lighthouse, watching the whales out there weave gracefully in and out of the needle-sharp rocks.

Hal was somewhere out there, he knew, but there was no way that he could reach him. The tourists who had taken Blaise's powerboat had still not returned from their trip along the coast to Saint Michael's Mount, which meant that the Pendragon Lighthouse was a no-go area for them.

'Couldn't you take one of the fishing boats?' Colette suggested after she had returned from Kim's hostel, where the older girl had tried to alert the coastguard and had met with the failure that Marc knew she would have.

'We'd be smashed against the rocks,' Marc said. 'Hal's beaten us. He's probably miles away by now.'

Suddenly the two of them heard the distinctive sound of helicopter blades coming from the east. They both looked in the direction of Lyonesse island.

'Broderick Rune,' Colette guessed, and then frowned. The helicopter seemed to be following something in the water.

'It's Rebecca!' Marc said as he recognised the distinctive livery of one of Blaise's speedboats and Rebecca's even more distinctive mane of auburn hair, which was blowing in the wind.

'Something's wrong!' Colette said.

They watched on in horror as the low-flying helicopter buzzed down on Rebecca, who was trying desperately to outmanoeuvre her pursuer. Suddenly the air was full of the sound of gunfire, and the waters around the powerboat were churned with tiny explosions.

'They're shooting at her!' Colette realised. 'What are they trying to do? Kill her?'

'Obviously,' came back Marc's worried response. 'And there's nothing we can do to help her!'

Dateline: Balan's Bay;
Thursday 27 August; 16.18.

Rebecca looked up desperately as the helicopter loomed ever closer, and she tried to steer the boat to land. Malvaine was leaning out of the passenger window, smiling maliciously at her, as he fired into the waters around the boat. He had only been playing with her so far, teasing her as a cat does with a mouse, but soon, she knew, he would move in for the kill.

She glanced forward and wiped the spray from her eyes, which stung with its salt tanginess. Directly ahead of her was Balan's Bay. If she could just reach there, then she might just be able to hide behind the rocks which dotted the bay. She increased the speed of the powerboat. There wasn't much time left.

The boat scrunched to a halt in Balan's Bay. Rebecca leapt out and started running across the sand. She looked up.

Malvaine and the helicopter had wheeled away from her, and were even now returning to Lyonesse island. It seemed that they had given up their chase. Rebecca wondered why.

For a short half-instant, her thoughts turned to why she was finding it so enormously difficult to move.

Then she remembered.

Quicksand!

The sands of Balan's Bay were slowly dragging her down. Malvaine had known that: that was why he had left her here.

The sands had already reached her knees and were slowly sucking her down. Rebecca panicked and tried to pull her legs out. She fell flat on her face, as the sands dragged her ever downwards. She tried to reach out for something – a rock, a branch, anything. But there was nothing.

The quicksands of Balan's Bay were about to claim their next victim.

Dateline: Arthur's Bay;
Thursday 27 August; 16.21.

'She's going under!' Colette said, as they raced along the beach towards Balan's Bay. 'We'll never reach her in time.'

Marc knew with a heavy heart that Colette was right. Soon the quicksands would claim Rebecca as their own. He looked over the sea, past the windsurfers, and towards Pendragon Rock. If only Hal hadn't taken the powerboat then they could have–

Windsurfers! Of course! That was it!

'There's only one way we can save Rebecca now!' he said and raced down to the shore, where one of the surfers was just preparing to launch. A rapid conversation followed, and then Marc took hold of the surfboard and rig and dragged it down into the water.

Hal had said that he had improved vastly in the past couple of days, Marc remembered, as he pulled himself up on the board, and started dragging the sail towards him, hoping that there was enough wind to catch. Now, as he started to speed off towards Balan's Bay it was his time to prove it!

Dateline: Balan's Bay;
Thursday 27 August; 16.24.

This is it, Rebecca realised, as the sands reached up to her shoulders, and the mud which she'd already swallowed made it difficult to breathe. She clawed out once more, trying desperately to grab hold of something solid, but the sand just yielded beneath her touch, and dragged her deeper and deeper down into its deadly embrace. It pressed tightly on her chest, crushing her, squeezing the very life out of her.

The world was spinning sickeningly around her. Her vision was becoming blurred. Hallucinating, she saw a brightly-coloured shape skip across the waves towards her. Those waves and the sea were little more than a metre away from her, but as far as she was concerned they might as well be further away than the moon. The unforgiving quicksands would not release her. She was theirs now, theirs for all eternity. A drowsiness fell upon Rebecca, as she finally stopped struggling.

'That's it, Bec,' a voice sounded in her head. Surely it wasn't Marc? 'Stop moving. The more you struggle, the more you'll sink. Stay calm.'

Marc manoeuvred the windsurfing board as far into the shallows as he dared. Then he carefully lowered the rig down so it was almost level with the sand – a few tantalising inches away from Rebecca's outstretched hand.

'Reach for the boom, Bec!' he called out, referring to the long central pole which supported the sail.

'I can't . . .' she spluttered.

No matter how hard she tried the boom was always just out of reach.

'Of course you can!' Marc encouraged her, but didn't dare bring the boom any lower.

Rebecca stretched out again and her fingers brushed lightly against the boom – before the sands pulled her away again.

'It's no use, Marc . . . it's impossible.' She felt herself sinking again.

'Of course it's possible!' Marc called out, not so encouragingly this time. 'Don't be such a wimp, Rebecca. Don't be such a *girl*!'

Rebecca glared at Marc. 'Just you wait till I get my hands on you, Marc Price!' she said through gritted teeth, and stretched out once more for the boom until it seemed that her arms would be ripped out of their sockets. 'I'll show you who's a wimp or not!'

Summoning up her very last reserves of strength, Rebecca reached out and finally managed to grab hold of the windsurfing boom. Marc let forth with a cry of triumph and slowly pulled the boom up, easing Rebecca out of the quicksand.

When she was finally free and was lying across the windsurfing board, panting for breath, Rebecca looked up at Marc. He was grinning from ear to ear.

'Well done, Bec!' he said. 'I knew you could do it!'

'You pig! You tricked me!'

'And I saved your life as well,' he reminded her.

'Marc, we have to go to Pendragon Rock!' Rebecca remembered.

'I know – that's where Hal is,' he said.

'Hal?' Rebecca didn't understand. 'No, we have to get to the Holy Grail before Broderick Rune does. We have to stop him gaining the secret of eternal life!'

THE PSYCHIC ZONE

9

Alien Sea

Dateline: Pendragon Rock;
Thursday 27 August; 18.30.

The weather had taken a turn for the worse, but now Rebecca was steering Blaise's power boat towards the rocks surrounding Pendragon Rock and its old lighthouse. There was a storm on the way, Blaise had told them, and he wouldn't be held responsible for what might happen to them in this weather. At which Marc had riposted that he didn't have to come with them if he didn't want to. Blaise had taken him up on the offer, and so it was that only Marc, Rebecca and Colette were making the perilous journey to the Rock.

Rebecca cut the engine. They were still some distance out from Pendragon Rock. She shook her head sadly.

'It's no use, Marc,' she said. 'We daren't go in any closer. One false move on my part and we could be smashed to pieces against those rocks. I don't know the area that well enough.'

'Maybe not,' said Colette and pointed delightedly to the starboard side of the boat. A school of killer whales was accompanying them towards Pendragon Rock, the whales' black dorsal fins proud and erect as they cut a path through the frothing waters around the lighthouse.

'I don't believe it,' said Marc as he peered over the side. 'They're guiding us through the rocks!'

'They must be the some of the ones that Joey made Broderick Rune release,' Rebecca said, as she powered up the engine again, and followed their aquatic guides.

'Kim always said that they were just as intelligent as humans,' Marc remembered.

'Let's hope they get us to Pendragon Rock safely,' Rebecca said. 'It's crucial that we reach the Grail cup before Rune does. Joey can't delay him forever . . .'

Dateline: Broderick Rune's Control Chamber, Lyonesse; Thursday 27 August; 18.34.

'Are you wasting my time, boy?' Broderick Rune snarled, as Joey studied the map of Penwyn-Mar for what must have been the hundredth time. They were all of them – Joey, Rune, Elenore, Morgana and Malvaine – huddled around the marble desk in Rune's control chamber

Joey looked up spitefully at the old man. For the past hour or so now he'd been pretending to be trying to get a psychic fix on the location of the Grail cup by studying the map of the area. Not that he needed to, of course. He'd known the location of the Grail cup ever since he had entered Elenore's mind.

'I am growing impatient, boy,' Rune said and looked over to Malvaine and gave him a silent nod. Malvaine grinned, and crossed over to Elenore. He grabbed her roughly and slipped a knife from out of his pocket, which he held to her throat. Elenore struggled, but the man was much too strong for her. There was a look of abject fear in her eyes.

'OK,' Joey said. 'Leave her alone.'

'Find me the Grail cup and I shall,' Broderick Rune said. 'Fail me and Malvaine will take the greatest pleasure in slitting her throat from ear to ear.'

Joey glowered at Rune and then turned all his attention back to the map. He closed his eyes and pretended to concentrate, 'dowsing' the map just as he knew Malvaine had seen him do at the site and Rune had spotted him at the minefield.

Finally, he took a deep breath, opened his eyes, and jabbed a grubby finger on the point marking the Pendragon lighthouse.

'There,' he said with finality. 'You'll find the Grail

buried under Pendragon Rock.'

Broderick Rune, Morgana and Malvaine all exchanged interested looks.

'It is one of the places we suspected,' Morgana said smugly. 'Pendragon was the name of Arthur's father.'

'Our bombs couldn't shift anything,' Malvaine remembered. 'It was a waste of some good whales.'

'If our explosives couldn't unearth anything, then whatever lies down there must be well protected indeed,' Broderick Rune decided. 'Malvaine, prepare the helicopter. I shall accompany the boy and the girl.'

Joey looked incredulously at Rune. 'You can't travel about on Pendragon Rock in a wheelchair,' he protested.

'I do not intend to,' Rune said, and Joey's incredulity turned to amazement as Broderick Rune eased himself out of his wheelchair and on to his own two legs. There was a look of intense distress on the billionaire's face. 'Artificial, biomechanical legs.' he explained. 'The pain is great, but not so great that it shall prevent me from gaining that which I most desire.'

'And when the Grail is all yours,' purred Morgana, 'then all your pain shall cease. And you shall be young and strong and vibrant again – forever.'

'Indeed,' said Rune. 'Now make all haste! The Grail cup must be mine!'

Dateline: Pendragon Rock;
Thursday 27 August; 19.16.

The approach to Pendragon Rock was smoother
and safer than Rebecca could ever have hoped for.
She moored the boat to an outlying rock, while
Colette walked back to the seashore waving at the
whales, as if to thank them.

'Colette, do you really think they understand
what you're saying to them?' Marc asked. He
himself liked to believe half-a-dozen impossible
things before breakfast, but even this was going a
little too far! He told her so.

'And why ever shouldn't they?' she asked.
'Rebecca's probably right. These are the whales that
Joey told her he'd had Broderick Rune release as a
condition of helping him.'

'And you honestly think that they know that
we're friends of his?'

'Watch,' Colette said superiorly, and reached into
the pocket of her jeans for the whistle that Kim had
given to her on the day they'd found the dead
Starshine. She blew a few toots on it. Nothing
happened.

'Am I supposed to be impressed?' Marc asked
cynically.

'They all have their individual call-signs,' Colette
said, and tried a different variation of the whistle
she'd originally piped: two shorts, followed by two
longs and then one more short.

This time one of the whales seemed to recognise the call. It stopped its gambolling with the other whales and swam over to Colette at the water's edge. It honked happily, and Colette patted it on its snout.

'You see?' she said smugly. 'They *are* as intelligent as we are. Or at least, as intelligent as *some* of us are!'

Marc ignored her last comment. 'And you think that I'm impressed?' he asked.

'Yes,' said Colette with a knowing grin.

Marc looked back at Rebecca, who had already secured the boat and was now checking out their surroundings. She pointed to another speedboat, moored quite close to theirs.

'He hasn't covered his tracks then,' she remarked as Marc and Colette came over to join her.

'Why should he?' Colette asked. 'No one ever comes to Pendragon Rock these days.'

'It's the rocks, I suppose,' Rebecca said. 'If it wasn't for the help of the whales, we'd've probably been smashed to pieces on them.'

'*And* the ghosts,' Colette said. 'Why do you think that the lighthouse is abandoned? You couldn't find a lighthouse keeper who'd stay here longer than a couple of months. They used to talk of water-demons who took on the shape of men.'

'And now we know who the water-demon is,' Marc said, but was contradicted by Rebecca, who was exploring the area just beyond Hal's speedboat.

'Do we?'

'Come on, Bec,' Marc protested as he came over to join her. 'If you'd've seen the trail of footprints that he left behind.'

'But I didn't,' she reminded them both. 'As far as I'm concerned, Hal's a perfectly nice guy.'

'So why did he steal the carcass of Kim's whale?' Colette asked pointedly.

'I don't know,' Rebecca admitted. 'So shall we find out?'

'How?' asked Colette.

'Well, while you two have been talking about water-demons and ghosts, I've been doing what a scientist like myself does best.'

'Being too intelligent for her own good?' Marc said, and then wished he hadn't as Rebecca darted him an evil look.

'No. Observing, and taking notice of things,' she said, and pointed to a group of rocks a few metres away from Hal's moored boat.

'So?' Marc said. 'I don't see anything.'

'Look closer,' Rebecca suggested.

Marc walked over to the group of rocks, most of which were even bigger than he was. They were all bare, except for two rocks which were covered with a thick expanse of seaweed.

'So?' Marc shrugged his shoulders. 'What's so special about them?' He asked Colette if she had noticed anything but she shook her head. As far as she was concerned, a rock was a rock was a rock.

'Look closer,' Rebecca said again. The two of

them did as they were asked, but still couldn't find anything out of the ordinary.

'C'mon, Bec, we both of us know that you're enjoying this!' Marc said, and Rebecca guessed, that, yes, maybe he was right. 'Put us out of our misery!'

'All the other rocks are bare,' she said, 'apart from these two.'

'So?' Colette still couldn't quite see where this was leading.

'So why these two?' Rebecca asked. She reached out and lifted the seaweed, and Marc and Colette gasped in amazement – and admiration. The seaweed had been concealing a cleft between the two rocks about a metre wide.

Rebecca looked to the north. A light was rapidly approaching them and already she could hear the distinctive sound of helicopter blades. 'We'd better hurry,' she said. 'Broderick Rune will be here soon.

Dateline: Pendragon Rock;
Thursday 27 August; 19.44.

The tunnel in which they found themselves was dark and narrow. They had to walk in single file, holding each others' hands; with Rebecca taking the lead, Colette in the middle, and Marc casting a wary look behind them for any sign of Broderick Rune.

'That's the way with tunnels,' Marc said cheerfully in the darkness. 'They're dark and narrow so that, when you meet the nasty at the other end, it's gonna be one hell of a problem to run away from it.'

'Thank you so much,' Colette said, sarcastically. She hated darkness and confined spaces. 'I'd rather not think about things like that.'

'Yes, don't be an idiot, Marc,' Rebecca scolded, and then turned to Colette. Even in the half-light she could see the look of fear on her face. 'And don't worry – there won't be any "nasties" at the end of this tunnel, as Marc calls them.'

'You can't be certain of that,' Colette said, hoping that Rebecca couldn't detect the note of fear in her voice.

'Oh yes I can,' Rebecca said, confidently. 'We've reached a dead end.'

'We can't have done,' Marc said. The tunnel widened out a little where he was standing and he pushed past the two girls to take a look. Sure enough, Rebecca was right. There was nowhere else to go.

'It's impossible,' he said. 'Hal must have gone down here.'

'How?' Rebecca asked. 'As well as being a water-demon, I suppose he's also able to walk through walls?'

Marc looked thoughtfully the tunnel wall for a moment. 'Oh no, he didn't,' he said finally, and pointed to the chink of light which was shining down on all their faces. 'What's blocking our way isn't a wall at all!'

Rebecca peered more closely into the darkness and found that Marc was right. A large boulder was blocking their progress, sealing off the rest of the tunnel.

'You're right,' she said, a little begrudgingly.

'Of course I am, Bec,' Marc chuckled, pleased at last to have got his own back. 'How do you think we can still see each other in the darkness? I'm a scientist. I *observed*.'

'OK, point taken,' Rebecca said, smiling to herself in the darkness. 'Now what do we do?'

Marc sighed theatrically and made an exaggerated point of flexing his muscles. 'Brain power is all very well, *girls*–' he began pompously.

'You call me a girl again in that tone of voice and I'll throttle you!' Rebecca warned.

Marc smiled, shaking his head. 'But there are times when sheer brute force is all you really need!'

Dateline: Pendragon Rock;
Thursday 27 August; 19.58.

At the very moment that Marc was attempting to move the boulder that was blocking his and the girls' path, Broderick Rune's helicopter was finally touching down on Pendragon Rock.

The first to jump out of the chopper was Malvaine. Strapped over his shoulder was a long-barrelled weapon, the likes of which Joey had never seen before. A product of Broderick Rune's computer empire, he guessed, and, from the way that Malvaine cradled it almost lovingly, it was obviously a weapon of enormous power and destruction. Malvaine also had an enormous backpack slung over his shoulders, and Joey and Elenore both wondered what it might contain.

Morgana followed him out, and, with the gun that Rune had provided for her, she ushered out Joey and Elenore as well. Elenore was by now as white as a sheet, and Joey had been stunned by the change in her appearance and attitude since they had left Lyonesse. She looked like a woman condemned to the executioner's chamber, and Joey felt a twinge of guilt. If only he could tell her what he had learnt when he had linked his mind to hers. But if he did that, then who could tell what the reaction of the woman who called herself Elenore Morgan would be?

Broderick Rune was the last to leave the helicopter. He moved jerkily on his two artificial, biomechanical legs, and the pain on his face was evident for all to see. Still, when Madame Morgana reached out a hand to help and steady him, he pushed her away.

'Forget me!' he snarled. From the air, he had spotted Rebecca, Marc and Colette find the entrance to Hal's hidden tunnel. 'The Grail is all that matters. Eternal life must – *will* – be mine!'

Dateline: Pendragon Rock;
Thursday 27 August; 20.09.

'OK, big boy, I have to say that I'm impressed,'
Rebecca said, with the sort of sarcasm that only a
native New Yorker could ever muster.

'Sometimes you need brawn as well as brains,'
Marc said, as he wiped the sweat from his brow. It
had been quite an effort to move the stone away
from the entrance and every one of his muscles was
aching. Heck, he was even aching in places where
he didn't know that he had muscles!

Colette, however, wasn't interested in the two
friends' sparring. Instead, she had walked through
the concealed entrance that Marc had uncovered
and was now marvelling at the sight before her.
And what she saw quite simply took her breath
away.

The tunnel opened out into an enormous cavern,
the size, Colette guessed, of a small cathedral. She
took a step forwards and then reached out for the
sides of the tunnel wall to steady herself, and stop
herself from falling. Directly in front of her there
was a sheer drop. She gasped in horror. If she had
taken another step further, she would have fallen
some forty... fifty... sixty metres into the murky
depths of a subterranean sea – the limits of which
she couldn't make out, even in the weird green light
which flooded the cavern and almost blinded her
eyes with its unearthly brilliance.

'An underground ocean!' Marc said. 'I've heard of stuff like this but I never knew they really existed. Where's the light coming from? Whatever it is, it's hurting my eyes.'

'Some sort of natural phosphorescence,' Rebecca guessed.

'Phospho-what?' asked Colette. 'Sorry, but all this scientific stuff is beyond me.'

'Certain minerals in certain kinds of rocks absorb light or energy and then reflect it back,' Rebecca said knowledgeably, recalling her physics lessons.

'But what kind of energy could create this sort of light?' Colette asked. 'It's so bright it's hurting my eyes.'

'Something *alien*,' Marc said, ominously.

'Shall we find out?' Rebecca asked.

'But how?' said Colette. 'It's a sheer drop down below.'

'No, it's not,' said Rebecca.

There was a kind of small rocky ledge just to the right-hand side of the tunnel-opening. From that ledge a rope bridge stretched to the far side of the cavern wall, where another ledge ran the length of the wall and into the shadows.

'We climb across *that*?' Colette asked warily. She looked down at the churning waters of the alien sea and then back at the rope bridge. It looked decidedly unsafe. 'We're not even sure where it leads to.'

'It has to lead somewhere,' Marc said reasonably as he set his foot on the bridge, which started to sway worryingly under his weight. 'Otherwise why put it here in the first place?'

Slowly Marc, Colette and Rebecca made their way across the bridge, which swayed and creaked as they proceeded. In this damp atmosphere, the ropes were wet and rotten. Colette prayed that they would hold their combined weight. If not – well, when she looked down at the dark and deep waters of the alien sea, she decided that she'd prefer not to think what would happen to her.

A shot rang out in the cavern, echoing and re-echoing among the rocks.

Rebecca cast a wary look behind her: Broderick Rune and the others had just entered the tunnel, and she cursed herself for not having the foresight to have asked Marc to roll the stone back, thereby giving themselves some valuable time.

'Turn back!' she heard Broderick Rune call out. 'Turn back now or we kill the boy!'

'We have to go back!' Colette said as she stumbled on the rope bridge, nearly losing her balance. She reached out to Marc for support and almost knocked him over as well.

'No, we must keep going!' Rebecca said, and pushed Colette further forwards. 'He daren't kill Joey: otherwise he'll never be able to locate the Grail.'

Rebecca was right, and Marc grabbed hold of Colette's hand and dragged her across the bridge and on to the ledge at the far side of the cavern. When all three of them were safely on the other side, he reached into the back pocket of his jeans and pulled out a penknife.

'What do you think you're planning to do with that?' Rebecca asked incredulously.

'Cut the rope bridge down,' he told her. 'That'll stop them from reaching us.'

'And cut off what's probably our only way of getting back to the surface!' Rebecca cried. 'Don't be a fool!'

But it was too late to do anything. Rune and the others had already reached the bridge. If Marc had cut it now, along with Rune, Malvaine and Morgana, Joey and Elenore would have fallen into that alien sea.

They raced along the ledge and into the shadows, trying hard not to look down into the waters far below them.

'Do you think that this sea's got something to do with the dying whales?' Marc gasped, and ducked as another bullet ricocheted off the cavern wall. He looked behind him at Morgana, who had fired the shot. She was dragging Elenore across the bridge with her, and, even at this distance, Marc could see the strangest expression on the archaeologist's face. She was staring blankly ahead, allowing herself to be guided by Morgana like a deaf, dumb and blind woman. Joey, who was being held by Malvaine, was kicking and struggling as he was being dragged along. Elenore, on the other hand, was putting up no resistance whatsoever.

Rune was halfway across the bridge by now.

There wasn't a moment to lose. Marc pointed out a series of stone steps which ran from the ledge and down to a small rocky promontory below which jutted out into the subterranean sea.

'Marc, these are *steps*,' Rebecca said, as she followed him and Colette down.

'Of course they are,' Marc said.

'They're not natural,' she said with foreboding. 'They were made by someone – or *something*.'

That jolted Marc and he came to an abrupt halt. His foot slipped and he almost fell some twenty metres into the waiting sea below. Colette reached and dragged him back from the edge.

'Thanks,' he said, and looked down at the sea. He could see tiny dots of black-and-white floating in the waters. Orcas, he guessed, who had somehow found their way in here from the surface sea. He was about to continue his descent down to the islet when he wrinkled his nose.

'What's up?' Rebecca asked, and cast a nervous glance behind her. Broderick Rune was gaining on them fast; this was no time to stop and make idle conversation, for heaven's sake!

'Smell,' Marc said, simply.

'What are you talking about?'

'Just smell.'

Rebecca and Colette frowned with puzzlement but nevertheless did as Marc instructed.

'It smells different!' Colette said. 'You know how whenever you're near the sea, you can always detect a sort of salty tanginess in the air?

This sea's different. This sea smells *sweet*!'

'Whatever's down there, it's like no sea we've ever seen before,' Marc said with growing unease.

'I'd like to point out that we have three homicidal maniacs on our trail,' Rebecca said practically, and pushed past the two of them. 'We can worry about this sea later.'

Colette and Marc followed her example, and within fifteen minutes or so they had reached the foot of the steps that had been carved out of the rocks.

They paused for a moment to examine their surroundings. The islet was little more than a rocky outcrop, jutting out from the cavern wall, surrounded by the sea. However, roughly two hundred metres away from them, they could sight land – or rather another part of the cavern wall. There was a large cleft cut into the rocks and from out of it an eerie green light was pulsing.

'That's where we're heading,' Marc decided.

'There isn't anywhere else for us to go,' Rebecca agreed. With Broderick Rune closing in on them with every second, their choices of escape were severely limited.

Colette looked warily across the water towards the baleful green light that seemed now to be pulsing in time with her own terrified heart. 'But how do we get there?' she asked them.

Marc shrugged, and kicked off his trainers. 'Swim, of course,' he said and walked to the water's edge.

'We can't!' Colette protested. 'We don't know how the water might affect us! And think of the whales!'

'We've no other choice,' Rebecca said, and started to remove her own shoes as well. 'Just make sure you don't swallow any of the water.'

'But the other side is so far away,' Colette objected. 'We'd never make it.'

'Do you want to wait for Broderick Rune to capture us then?' Marc snapped, losing his patience.

'No, I – but –' Colette hung her head in shame. 'But I can't swim . . .'

'Damn!' Rebecca cursed, and then apologised to Colette. 'I forgot about that.'

'You leave me here,' Colette said. 'I'll be all right . . .'

'Don't be ridiculous,' Rebecca said. She glanced up at the steps leading down to the islet. Rune, Malvaine, Morgana, Joey and Elenore were already halfway down, their progress only slowed by the large backpack and gun which Malvaine was carrying, and Broderick Rune's artificial legs.

Rebecca looked enquiringly at Marc. 'Do you think you can take her with you?' she asked, but they both knew that it would be impossible. Marc was a good swimmer, but not that good; and he knew that, if Colette panicked (and he wasn't sure whether she would or not), she might take them both down.

'Maybe I can't,' Marc said, 'but I know someone who might. Colette, take out your whistle.'

Colette did as she was told and tried a few experimental toots on it. For long seconds nothing happened . . . and then a snout broke the surface of the water, and an orca honked happily at them.

'It's one of the whales that Joey freed,' Colette realised.

'Do you think it can help us?' Rebecca asked Marc.

'Kim told us that they were more intelligent than human beings,' Marc said. 'Let's put it to the test, shall we?'

Colette walked to the edge of the islet and bent down on one knee. She reached a hand out to the killer whale and patted it gently on its snout. The orca gave a delighted squeak.

'That's it, Colette,' Rebecca said, encouragingly. 'Reach into its mind. Tell it what we want.'

Colette closed her eyes, trying to connect her mind with the orca's. She felt her consciousness slip into its consciousness; her being into its being. She had tried the same sort of thing with Joey occasionally and had met with only limited success. But now, in the presence of one of the creatures that some said were even more intelligent than mankind, she felt a joyful sensation of connecting, a mutual understanding that she had never experienced before. *Safety* – she repeated the word over and over in her mind, even as Broderick Rune and the others were getting nearer and nearer – *take us to safety . . . to safety . . . to safety . . .*

Marc and Rebecca watched on, fascinated. Was

Colette succeeding? Was it really a glimmer of understanding that they could see in the whale's tiny eyes?

Their questions were answered the very next second, as two more whales came up to join their fellow orca. They rolled over playfully in the water and waved their fins at Colette, Rebecca and Marc.

'Do you think they understand her?' Rebecca asked.

'There's only one way to find out, isn't there?' Marc said, and lowered himself into the water. He climbed on to the whale's back, keeping tight hold of its erect dorsal fin. Without further ado, the whale sped off from the shore and towards the pulsing green light at the far end of the cavern.

'Way to go, man! Way to go!' Joey cheered, as he watched Colette and Rebecca mount their own whales and speed off across the waters of the alien sea.

His joy was short-lived however, for, as soon as he reached the islet, Malvaine unshouldered his heavy backpack and took out what at first sight looked like just a tightly-packed bundle of plastic. He pulled on a cord attached to the plastic, and Joey and Elenore watched on, amazed, as the plastic bundle started slowly to inflate itself into a full-sized dinghy.

Another example of Broderick Rune's technology! Joey thought: technology which might soon win him the ultimate prize of the Holy Grail.

Marc, Rebecca and Colette were not safe yet from

Broderick Rune and his maniacal quest for the Holy Grail. And neither was the rest of the world.

Dateline: Alien Sea; Thursday 27 August; 21.19.

'Looks like we've lost them,' Marc said. The cleft in the rock, to which their three marine rides had taken them, had proved to be the opening to yet another tunnel, which seemed to lead even deeper into the earth.

'Don't speak too soon,' said Rebecca, who, like Marc and Colette, hadn't seen Malvaine set sail in the inflatable dinghy. 'Rune's obsessed with finding the Grail. Somehow I don't think he'd leave anything to chance.'

'Listen. Can you hear that?' asked Colette.

'Hear what?' asked Rebecca. All she could hear was the constant *drip-drip-drip* of water from somewhere close by – which was hardly surprising – and she told Colette so.

'No, not that,' Colette said. 'It's a rushing sound. Like a waterfall. Maybe I'm just imagining it . . . Can you hear it, Marc?'

But Marc wasn't listening, either to Colette or to the imagined sound of a waterfall. Instead, he was examining the walls of the tunnel down which they were walking. He ran his hand along the side of the wall. It was warm to the touch; not dank and wet as he would have imagined. And another thing too.

'They're perfectly smooth,' he told them.

'Maybe at some point this tunnel was flooded with water,' Colette suggested. 'Over the ages, moving water could have smoothed the walls down.

'Congratulations, Colette! You're starting to think like a scientist at long last,' Rebecca said.

'Is that a compliment?' Colette asked with a smile.

'Feel it, Bec,' Marc said, and took Rebecca's hand and placed it against the smoothness of the tunnel wall. 'It might look like rock, but it sure as hell isn't.'

'It's metal,' Rebecca realised with growing wonder.

'And it's also a dead end,' Colette said gloomily, and Marc and Rebecca looked in the direction in which she was pointing.

Sure enough they were faced with a blank wall. Colette turned despairingly back to the others. 'That's it,' she said. 'We can't go any further.'

'It doesn't make sense,' Marc said. 'Why build a tunnel that goes nowhere? . . . Bec, what are you doing?'

'Coming up with an answer,' Rebecca said superiorly. She was on her knees and examining two panels made of stone – or *metal*, she corrected herself – which were set into the wall. 'Come and have a look at this.'

Marc and Colette joined her by the wall.

The first panel was rectangular and divided into two rows of five squares each. Each square contained one of the Roman numerals from one to ten. 'So whoever made this can count,' Marc said, flippantly. 'Big deal.'

'Now look at the other panel,' Rebecca said. This panel was also divided into two rows of five. Marc and Colette frowned as they read the numbers on these squares.

I	IV	VII	IX	XI
IX	XIV	XVI	IXX	

The final square was left blank.

'One, four, seven, nine, eleven, twelve, fifteen, sixteen, twenty,' Marc read out the numbers. 'I don't get it.'

Colette nodded her head in agreement. 'There's no sequence to the numbers,' she said.

'Maybe it's some sort of code?' Rebecca suggested.

'Well, whatever it is, we don't have the key for it,' Marc said, and continued to look at the Roman numerals. Slowly a look of realisation dawned on his face. 'Hydrogen, helium and lithium!'

'What?' Colette was none the wiser.

'The Periodic Table!' Marc said, excited now. 'These are the atomic weights, to the nearest whole number, of the first nine elements on the Periodic Table!'

'Of course!' said Rebecca, and kicked herself for not having realised the answer on her own.

'So why the blank square?' Colette asked.

'That must be for the tenth element in the Table,' Rebecca realised. She turned to Marc. 'You're the chemist, Marc. What is it?'

'Neon,' he said. 'The tenth element is neon.'

'And its atomic weight?'

Marc closed his eyes and tried to recall the exact figure. 'Twenty point one seven nine,' he remembered.

'Twenty then. Two times ten.' Rebecca went to the first panel and pressed the 'X' square twice.

For a moment nothing happened. And then they heard the whirring of machines, the purring of an engine, and the entire wall slid upwards into the roof.

'Not *another* tunnel,' Marc said.

'No, it opens up further on,' Colette said.

As they started to walk off down the tunnel, they were so full of anticipation that they didn't hear the entrance slide shut behind them.

'I didn't know that the people of King Arthur's time knew about the elements,' Colette said.

'They didn't,' said Rebecca.

Marc, who was taking up the lead, looked around him. 'You know what this tunnel reminds me of, Bec?' he asked.

'You tell me,' she said. 'As far as I'm concerned one tunnel looks very much like any other.'

'An airlock,' Mac said. 'But an airlock to where?'

And then they reached the end of the tunnel, and entered what, to all appearances, was a room of dead men.

THE PSYCHIC ZONE

10

Forever Young

Dateline: Alien Sea;
Thursday 27 August; 22.22.

The whole place reeked of death and decay. The tunnel – or airlock, as Marc had called it – opened up into what Rebecca could only describe as a tomb. It reminded Colette of her worst nightmare: when she was lost and trapped in a graveyard and the figures of the dead had arisen from their mausoleums.

About sixty or so figures were standing in the room in a series of concentric circles. Each of them stood on his or her own plinth, the bases of which were hidden in the greenish mist which billowed around the floor, and which was the source of the noisome stench. The smell reminded them all of something, but none of them could yet put a name to it.

Some plinths were vacant, as though waiting for their occupants. Colette counted three and wondered whether they had been reserved for her and Marc and Rebecca.

The figures on the plinths all stared ahead with blank and sightless eyes. Were they dead or alive? If they had registered Marc, Rebecca and Colette's entry into the room then they certainly didn't show it. They might have been statues if not for the fact that when Marc summoned up the courage to look closely at one, he could see that his chest was moving very slowly up and down.

'What are they?' whispered Colette, as she took Rebecca's arm for reassurance and they approached the nearest figure. He was a tall and imposing man with a long white beard, horrible dead eyes, and dressed in what appeared to be some sort of chain-mail armour. For a moment Colette was reminded of the legends of King Arthur, supposedly asleep in some secret location, waiting for the time when his country should need him and he would awake once again to lead them into battle. She looked at Rebecca. 'Is he really King Arthur?'

'Of course not,' Rebecca said, although there was some uncertainly in her voice. 'Arthur was a war chief, nothing more.'

'Some of these guys aren't even human,' Marc said as he weaved his way in-between the bodies, and towards one of the inner circles.

Short, grey creatures, with long spindly limbs and wide, bulbous eyes: dead eyes. Tall, proud and regal-looking characters, dressed in what could have been armour or could just as easily have been spacesuits. The same dead eyes. Horrible monstrosities. Dead eyes. Bird-men. Women with flippers instead of limbs. Dead eyes; dead eyes; everywhere dead eyes; which nevertheless seemed to follow Marc, Rebecca and Colette around the chamber.

'What is this place?' Rebecca asked.

'Whatever it is, it's horrible,' Colette said. 'Let's get out of here!'

For the first time Rebecca managed to drag her eyes away from the awful figures and their dead eyes, and took in the rest of the chamber.

There were banks of hi-tech equipment and gridded monitors, screens which displayed a series of pulsing lights and regularly oscillating lines. A deep and sonorous *thump-thump thump-thump* sound filled the air, in time with the pulsating green light they had seen from the alien sea.

The sound reminded Colette of something and it took her a while to realise what it was. 'It's like a heartbeat,' she finally said.

'You know, I've got a really weird feeling that I know what this place is,' Rebecca said.

'What?'

Before Rebecca had time to reply, Marc called them over. He had moved out of the circle of the living-dead figures and had walked over to a tiny alcove in the corner of the chamber.

There, half-hidden by the shadows and the foul-smelling mists – *What did that smell remind them of?* they all wondered to themselves – was a large basin, fed by a stream of sweet-smelling water which was pouring in through a special filter set high in the roof. Was that the sound that Colette had heard outside?

Rebecca looked up. The roof was transparent, and through it she could see the killer whales and other marine animals swimming in the subterranean depths of the alien sea. For a moment she had a brief flash of panic as she imagined just how many hundreds of thousands of tons of water must be above her. And then she realised that the transparent ceiling was a product of some alien technology and she was in no danger at all.

'Bec, stop looking up there,' Marc said. 'Come and take a look at this!'

Rebecca went and joined him and Colette by the basin. And what she saw took her breath away.

'It can't be!' she said, refusing – for the first time ever – to believe in the evidence of her own eyes. 'It's just a myth, a legend . . .'

Standing in the centre of the basin was a golden chalice studded with rubies and emeralds and sapphires, overflowing with the water which was pouring down on it from the alien sea.

The Grail cup. Overflowing with the waters of eternal life itself.

'Broderick Rune was right,' Colette said in a reverent whisper. 'It does exist.'

'The secret of eternal life,' Marc said.

'We've no proof of that,' Rebecca said automatically, and then stopped herself. *This is the real thing*, her heart told her, and for once her head had reluctantly to agree. They had stumbled upon the one thing that mankind had been searching for through down the ages: the solution to all the ills and all the harms in the world.

'We don't need proof,' Marc said, and reached out, with a trembling hand, for the Grail chalice.

'Don't touch it.'

Marc drew his hand from the Grail cup as if he had been burnt, and they all turned to see – standing in a doorway at the far end of the chamber – Hal.

But it was a Hal who was vastly changed from the windsurfer they had all known back in Penwyn-Mar and Arthur's Bay. His long black hair was now tied back in a pony-tail – *very hygienic*, Rebecca thought, as her suspicion of a few moments ago was confirmed – and now at long last they could see the two slits on either side of his neck. *No, not slits*, realised Marc as Hal approached them, *but gills!*

Hal was no longer wearing his familiar outfit of a wet suit. Instead he was wearing a white tunic. And where once no one had seen him without his trainers or windsurfing boots, he now made no effort to disguise his webbed feet.

'You're not human, are you?' Marc said.

There was the trace of a smile on Hal's face. 'Obviously not,' he said.

'What are you doing here?' Colette asked. 'Why are you killing the whales? Why did you steal Starshine's body?'

'To destroy the evidence,' Hal said simply, without any trace of guilt in his voice. 'If Kim had examined the whale's carcass then she would have called in the authorities. I can't afford to draw attention to myself.' He indicated the other figures in the room, their dead eyes staring straight ahead. 'Or to the others. That is why I manufactured the lights which appeared over Pendragon Rock: to make people think that the lighthouse and Pendragon Rock were haunted.'

'What is this place?' Colette asked. 'It's evil.'

Hal raised an eyebrow in surprise. 'Evil?' he asked. 'Is that what you really think, Colette? Or is it just what you've been taught?'

Colette remembered the stories Blaise had told her as a child. *Evil dwells at Penwyn-Mar*, he'd say, while Aunt Annie would wonder why, if evil dwelt there, the villagers always remained in the best of health and Dr Monmouth was more or less out of a job.

'I don't know,' she said truthfully.

'It's just a story,' Hal continued, 'like the stories of King Arthur.'

'But not like the stories of the Holy Grail,' Marc said, and nodded back to the chalice overflowing with its life-giving waters. 'Colette asked you what this place is. Tell us – what is it? And who are you?'

Hal smiled, a friendly smile which Marc didn't

entirely trust. 'It's very simple, Marc,' he began. 'This place is a–'

Suddenly there was an almighty explosion from the entrance to the tunnel, and the air became black with dense clouds of smoke.

Broderick Rune! They had all forgotten about him! Was it the effect of those green mists? And why did that smell seem so familiar still?

Malvaine was the first to enter the chamber, the super-powered gun he had used to blast down the airlock door still smoking. Morgana was next, dragging Joey and Elenore with her, and, following them, came Broderick Rune himself, moving as fast as his artificial legs would carry him.

Joey gave Marc, Rebecca and Colette a sheepish look. 'Hi, guys,' he said, a little guiltily. 'I tried to stall them as much as I could.'

'It doesn't matter, Joey,' Rebecca said, and then looked at Elenore. Her face was white and her lips were trembling, but there was a look of recognition in her eyes.

Hal ignored Rune and the others and instead smiled at Elenore. 'Welcome home, Elenore,' he said in a kindly voice. 'I've been looking for you for a long time. I was very worried about you.'

Joey looked up at Elenore. 'Elenore, what is he talking about?' he asked.

'I know now,' she said in a hushed whisper, as she looked around the chamber. She recognised the standing figures, their eyes dead and unseeing. She recognised the Grail cup. She recognised Hal. And for the first time in many years, she recognised herself.

'I know at last,' she said. 'I know who I am!'

There was no time to ask Elenore any questions. Morgana's eyes had alighted on the Grail cup in the corner of the room. They grew wide with wonder. She had spun Broderick Rune many a story about the ancient legends of Britain, in the hope of squeezing ever more money out of the billionaire. Never had she ever believed that the Grail really did exist. She approached it in awe and wonder.

'Stay away from it, Morgana,' Broderick Rune warned her, but Morgana didn't seem to hear him.

'It exists,' she crooned softly to herself. 'It really exists.'

She reached out a heavily ringed hand to touch the chalice and, as she did so, a shot rang out. The hand of Madame Morgana never did touch the fabled Holy Grail, and she fell dead on the floor, merely inches away from it.

'You killed her,' Malvaine said.

'Yes,' said Broderick Rune. 'She had served her purpose. Just as you, Malvaine, have served yours.'

Broderick Rune fired point-blank at his smartly suited henchman who had served him for years, and Malvaine crumpled to the floor in a dead heap.

Broderick Rune now turned to Joey. He aimed his revolver at him.

'No one must know of the existence of the Grail but Broderick Rune,' he intoned, as his finger squeezed on the trigger. 'No one but Broderick

Rune must possess the secret of health and of eternal life. With that secret I can rule the world. With that secret I can become forever young.'

Joey stared defiantly at Rune. 'So fire ahead, buster! Like I'm scared!' he said, trying hard to conceal the fact that he was very scared indeed.

'Shut up, Joey!' Rebecca said. 'Can't you see the guy is mad?'

'No, he isn't mad,' said Hal, and started walking towards Broderick Rune. In his hands he was carrying the Grail cup, filled to the brim with its precious, life-giving fluid, the fluid that would cure Broderick Rune of all his ills and grant him eternal life. 'Take it, Broderick Rune,' Hal said, as he handed over the chalice to the billionaire. 'Take what is yours by right. Take what has been created for the likes of you. Drink of the waters of eternal life.'

'Hal! You can't give him the Grail cup!' Rebecca protested.

'He's tried to kill us all!' Joey said.

Marc moved forwards and tried to knock the Grail out of Rune's hand. But Hal was too quick for him. He grabbed hold of Marc's arm.

'The Grail is destined for Broderick Rune,' Hal said. 'For Broderick Rune and all those who are like him.'

'What do you mean?'

'Look,' said Hal. 'Look at Broderick Rune.'

There was something in Hal's manner which made Marc forget his anger towards the windsurfer and instead look at Rune. The billionaire was drinking deeply of the cup, gulping its life-giving waters down so greedily that the liquid dribbled down his chin and fell to the floor.

'Do you enjoy your gift of eternal life, Broderick Rune?' Hal asked.

'It feels so beautiful,' Rune said ecstatically, and, to Marc, Rebecca, Joey and Colette, Broderick Rune somehow seemed a different man: younger, stronger, more vital.

For a moment, that was. And then the Grail chalice fell from Broderick Rune's crabbed and ancient hands, clattering to the metal floor and spilling out its life-giving contents. Broderick Rune looked at Hal, who was watching him sadly. 'Take it, Broderick Rune,' Hal said. 'Take the only immortality the likes of you can ever know.'

Broderick Rune stiffened and Colette thought for a moment that he was suffering a heart attack. And then she saw the glazed, dead look in his eyes, and realised that he had become just like the other people in the room. Alive – but dead.

'What's happened?' Rebecca said.

'It's some sort of suspended animation,' Joey said knowledgeably.

Marc, Rebecca and Colette all stared at him. 'How do you know that?' Marc asked.

'I read Elenore's mind,' Joey reminded them.

Everyone turned to Elenore who, in all the excitement, they had forgotten. She was cowering in a corner, looking at none of them, but staring with fascination at the Grail cup on the floor.

Hal reached out his hand for hers. She took it willingly. 'Are you ready now, Elenore?' he asked. Gently. Lovingly even.

Elenore nodded her head and followed Hal as he picked up the Grail cup, went over to the basin, and refilled it with the waters of the alien sea. He handed the cup to Elenore.

'Hey, now just wait a minute –' Marc said, but Joey held him back.

'No, big buddy,' he said softly. 'It's OK.'

Marc and the others watched on in horror as Elenore drank of the Grail cup. They expected her to freeze into immobility immediately, as had Broderick Rune, but instead she smiled and then walked through the green mists – *what was that smell?* – and to one of the empty plinths. She stood on top of it, and then her eyes glazed over and she moved no more.

'What's happened to her?' asked Colette.

'She is asleep,' Hal said simply. 'She will wake when there is a cure for her illness.'

'Her illness?' asked Marc. 'What illness?'

Hal chose not to answer his question. Instead he looked at Rebecca. 'You've guessed, haven't you?'

Rebecca nodded. 'I think so,' she said. 'This place is like a hospital, isn't it?'

'Yes,' Hal replied. 'A hospital for the mentally ill.'

That smell, Marc and Colette suddenly realised. The smell of *hospitals* ... They looked at Hal's clothes: the white tunic; the hair, tied hygienically back in a pony-tail revealing his gills – which left them in no doubt now that he wasn't human.

'And you, you're some sort of doctor,' Colette realised.

'Elenore was my patient,' Hal said, and then indicated the others standing there in their deathless sleep. 'As are all of these. But she didn't succumb to the effects of the Grail cup in the same way as the others. She awoke and escaped. It was only when the microcircuit was discovered, and it sent out its homing beacon, that she came back to Penwyn-Mar – came back to me.'

'But the dead whales?' Colette asked. 'Why did you kill the whales?'

'I didn't,' Hal said. 'That was Broderick Rune's fault.'

'Rune?' Marc looked over at the lifeless figure of the aged billionaire, immobile now for all eternity. 'How was he responsible for the dead whales?'

'The explosions he caused around Pendragon Rock in his search for the Grail,' Hal said. 'They caused a breach in the seabed and allowed the waters of the alien sea to filter into the sea around Penwyn-Mar.'

'I still don't understand,' Rebecca said.

'When my people first came here, they altered the chemical composition of the subterranean sea,' Hal told them. 'They transformed it in such a way that if any biped should drink its water then they would fall into a dreamless sleep.'

Rebecca remembered her advice to Marc and Colette not to swallow the water. She hadn't known it at the time but it had probably been the best advice she had ever given anyone.

'But mixed with the salt water of the surface sea, the results could be terrible,' Hal continued, with genuine regret. 'All mammals, even the whales, would suffer terrible genetic mutations. But they're safe, now that I have healed the breaches in the sea walls.'

'Your midnight swims,' Colette recalled. 'That was what you were doing.' Hal nodded.

Joey looked at the unseeing figures of Elenore and Broderick Rune and all the others in the chamber. 'What will happen to them?' he asked.

'When a cure for their illnesses is found they will be revived and sent back to their respective home worlds,' Hal told them, and walked up to the body of Broderick Rune. 'Although for some I fear that their illnesses will be incurable.'

'He was – is – a very old guy, I guess,' Joey said.

'His physical illnesses are not the ones I was talking about,' Hal said with a sad half-smile. 'His mind is dominated by greed and the lust for power. Such ills are very hard to cure. Perhaps they never can be cured.'

He looked sadly at Broderick Rune and at Elenore, and then at the dead bodies of Malvaine and Morgana on the floor. 'Sometimes I think that even when a cure is found for all the diseases on your world, greed will still prove to be your species' downfall. Can I trust even you to keep my existence here a secret?'

Rebecca looked at Marc, Colette and Joey in turn. They each nodded at her.

The alien sea was one of the greatest scientific discoveries of the age. Final and conclusive evidence that alien civilisations did exist. A chemically-augmented sea that could send bodies into suspended animation until a cure could be found for their ailments. If they revealed its location, they would be heralded as latter-day Louis Pasteurs or Madame Curies. Honours would be heaped on them from every country in the world. The Nobel Prize would be theirs for the asking.

And Hal's work in caring for his patients would be ruined. His technology would be unscrupulously exploited by the Broderick Runes of this world. When you looked at it like that then there was only one decision they could make. Joey stepped forward and spoke for all of them.

'The alien sea is gonna be our secret,' he promised Hal. 'If anyone hears about it, it sure won't be from the four of us.'

Hal smiled and reached out and shook Joey's hand. 'Thank you, Joey,' he said. 'Now my work can carry on undisturbed.'

They all turned to go, but, before they did, Marc looked at Hal.

'Thanks for the windsurfing lessons,' he said.

'No problem.'

'But you're not really a windsurfer, are you?

'Of course not,' Hal agreed. 'That was merely an alias I used on land while I waited for Elenore to return.'

'And I used to think you were just a few years older than me,' Marc continued. 'But you're much older than that, as well, aren't you?'

'Of course,' Hal said. 'My people first decided over fifteen hundred years ago that this subterranean sea was perfectly suited for their requirements.'

'Fifteen hundred years ago,' Rebecca said, and stroked her chin thoughtfully. The time of Arturius, the *dux bellorum* of the British. The time when all the legends had started. A wild idea came to her, but it was Colette who asked the question.

'And your real name – it isn't Hal?'

'Of course not,' Hal replied.

'Then who are you really?' Joey asked, even though deep down he already knew the answer. 'What's your real name?'

'Merlin,' said Hal, and, with a smile, returned to his work.

BOOK 2
CHANGELINGS

Mathew Stone

The Institute is a school for brilliant young scientists, but even Marc, Rebecca, Joey and Colette can't explain away some weird and sinister events . . .

A plane crashes but there are no bodies found. At the same time, people are mysteriously disappearing on Darkfell Rise and a comet is coming ever closer to Earth. Could there be a link between all these events and Colette's strange new friends . . ?

Paranormal? Or a cover up? The truth lies in the psychic zone . . .

BOOK 1
MINDFIRE

Mathew Stone

The Institute is a school for brilliant young scientists, but even Marc, Rebecca, Joey and Colette can't explain away some weird and sinister events . . .

A ball of flames sets part of the Institute on fire, but this is no accident. For clearly burnt into the ground is the eerie outline of a fox. Could this be anything to do with an ancient curse laid on the old Abbey – where the Institute now stands . . ?

Paranormal? Or a cover up? The truth lies in the psychic zone . . .

THE PSYCHIC ZONE

ORDER FORM

0 340 69836 5	MINDFIRE	£3.99 ☐
0 340 69840 3	CHANGELINGS	£3.99 ☐
0 340 69841 1	ALIEN SEA	£3.99 ☐

All Hodder Children's books are available at your local bookshop or newsagent, or can be ordered direct from the publisher. Just tick the titles you want and fill in the form below. Prices and availability subject to change without notice.

Hodder Children's Books, Cash Sales Department, Bookpoint, 39 Milton Park, Abingdon, OXON, OX14 4TD, UK. If you have a credit card you may order by telephone – 01235 831700.

Please enclose a cheque or postal order made payable to Bookpoint Ltd to the value of the cover price and allow the following for postage and packing:
UK & BFPO – £1.00 for the first book, 50p for the second book, and 30p for each additional book ordered up to a maximum charge of £3.00.
OVERSEAS & EIRE – £2.00 for the first book, £1.00 for the second book, and 50p for each additional book.

Name ....

Address ....

....

....

If you would prefer to pay by credit card, please complete:
Please debit my Visa/Access/Diner's Card/American Express (delete as applicable) card no:

Signature ....

Expiry Date ....